SONS OF

The
WARRIOR

a novella

ENCOURAGEMENT

FRANCINE RIVERS

TYNDALE HOUSE PUBLISHERS, INC.
WHEATON, ILLINOIS

Visit Tyndale's exciting Web site at www.tyndale.com

TYNDALE is a registered trademark of Tyndale House Publishers, Inc.

Tyndale's quill logo is a trademark of Tyndale House Publishers, Inc.

Check out the latest about Francine Rivers at www.francinerivers.com

"Seek and Find" section written by Peggy Lynch.

Edited by Kathryn S. Olson

Designed by Alyssa Force

Library of Congress Cataloging-in-Publication Data

Rivers, Francine, date.
  The warrior / Francine Rivers.
    p. cm. — (Sons of encouragement ; #2)
  ISBN 0-8423-8266-6
  1. Caleb (Biblical figure)—Fiction. 2. Bible. O.T.—History of Biblical events—Fiction.
I. Title. II. Series.
  PS3568.I83165W37 2005
  813'.54—dc22   2004024580

Printed in the United States of America

10   09   08   07   06   05
9   8   7   6   5   4   3   2   1

To men of faith who serve
in the shadow of others.

✦　✦　✦

I want to thank Peggy Lynch for listening
to my ideas and challenging me to dig
deeper and deeper. I also want to thank
my editor, Kathy Olson, for all her hard
work on these projects, and the entire
Tyndale staff for all the work they do in
presenting these stories to readers.
It's a team effort all the way.

Thank you to all who have prayed
for me over the years and through
the course of this particular project.
May the Lord use this story to
draw people close to Jesus,
our beloved Lord and Savior.

DEAR READER,

This is the second of five novellas on biblical men of faith who served in the shadows of others. These were Eastern men who lived in ancient times, and yet their stories apply to our lives and the difficult issues we face in our world today. They were on the edge. They had courage. They took risks. They did the unexpected. They lived daring lives, and sometimes they made mistakes—big mistakes. These men were not perfect, and yet God in His infinite mercy used them in His perfect plan to reveal Himself to the world.

We live in desperate, troubled times when millions seek answers. These men point the way. The lessons we can learn from them are as applicable today as when they lived thousands of years ago.

These are historical men who actually lived. Their stories, as I have told them, are based on biblical accounts. For the facts we know about the life of Caleb, see the books of Numbers, Joshua, and the beginning of Judges.

This book is also a work of historical fiction. The outline of the story is provided by the Bible, and I have started with the information provided for us there. Building on that foundation, I have created action, dialogue, internal motivations, and in some cases, additional characters that I feel are consistent with the biblical record. I have attempted to remain true to the scriptural message in all points, adding only what is necessary to aid in our understanding of that message.

At the end of each novella, we have included a brief

study section. The ultimate authority on people of the Bible is the Bible itself. I encourage you to read it for greater understanding. And I pray that as you read the Bible, you will become aware of the continuity, the consistency, and the confirmation of God's plan for the ages— a plan that includes you. Caleb lived God's commandment in Deuteronomy 6:5: "You must love the Lord your God with all your heart, all your soul, and all your strength." May we show his passion and surrender in following our Lord and Savior, Jesus Christ.

Francine Rivers

BIBLE scholars differ in their opinions as to whether the Caleb whose genealogy is listed in 1 Chronicles 2 is the same Caleb who scouted out the Promised Land with Joshua in Numbers 13. We know that Caleb the scout had a daughter named Acsah (Joshua 15:16), and the Caleb of 1 Chronicles 2 also had a daughter named Acsah (2:49). This correspondence has prompted the author to choose, for the purposes of this story, the view that they are indeed the same person. With this interpretation, references to "Caleb, son of Jephunneh" are taken to mean "Caleb, descendent of Jephunneh."

"RUN!"

No one heard, so Kelubai put his fingers in his mouth and gave a shrill whistle. His relatives raised their heads. He pointed at the darkening sky. They looked up and stared. *"Find cover!"*

Men, women, and children dropped their hoes and scattered. Kelubai followed. Farthest out in Pharaoh's field, he had the longest distance to run. The black swirling clouds moved with frightening speed, casting a cold shadow over the land. Was it the great lion of God that let out such a rumbling roar from that blackness? Screaming, hands over their heads, people ran faster.

A shaft of jagged light flashed and struck the middle of the barley field. Flames shot up from the ground and the stalks of ripened grain caught fire. Something hard struck Kelubai in the head. Then another and another, like small pebbles hurled at him from an open hand. And the air grew cold, so cold his breath came like puffs of smoke as he panted. His lungs burned. Could he make it to cover before one of those bolts of fire struck him down? He reached his mud-brick house, swung the door shut, and leaned against it.

Gasping for breath, he saw his wife, Azubah, crouched in the corner, their two older sons cowering beside her as she held their third son squalling at her breast. His older boys, Mesha and Mareshah, stood wide-eyed but silent. Their mother, Kelubai's first wife, would not have been as quick to give in to hysteria. She had faced death—giving Mareshah life—with more fortitude than Azubah now showed in the face of this storm.

Tears streaked her frightened face. "What is that noise, Kelubai? What's happening?" Her voice kept rising until she was screaming even louder than the babe. *What's happening?*

He grasped her shoulders and gave her a hard shake. "Hush!" He let go of her and ran his hands over his sons' heads. "Be quiet." He kissed each of them. "Shhhh. Sit still." He gathered them all close, shielding them with his body. His own heart was flailing, threatening to burst its bonds of bone and flesh. Never had he felt such terror, but he needed to be calm for their sake. He fixed his mind upon his family, soothing, encouraging. "Shhhh . . ."

"Abba." His oldest son, Mesha, pressed closer, his fingers grasping Kelubai's robe. "Abba . . ."

Hard pounding came against the house, like a thousand fists hitting at once. Azubah ducked her head, seeking the shelter of his shoulder. Mesha pressed close. Hard white stones flew in through the window. Curious, Kelubai rose. When his wife and sons protested, he set Mesha beside Azubah. "Stay calm. See to Mareshah." Kelubai could not depend on Azubah to comfort them. They were not her sons, and she would always hold her own flesh and blood more dear.

"Where are you going?"

"I just want to see."

"Kelubai!"

He held up his hand, commanding her to silence. Edging across the room, he reached out to take up one of the stones. It was hard and cold. Turning it in his hand, he examined it. It became slippery. Frowning, perplexed, he put it to his mouth. He glanced back at his wife and sons. "Water!" He picked up several more and brought them to

Azubah and his sons. "Taste it." Only Mesha was willing. "It's water. Water hard as a stone!"

Shivering, Azubah pressed back farther into the corner. "What manner of magic is this?" When a burst of light exploded outside the window, she screamed; the boys cried hysterically. Kelubai snatched the blankets from the straw pallets and draped them over the children. "Stay down."

"You can't go out there. You'll be killed!"

He put his hand gently over her mouth. "Do not make matters worse, woman. Your fear is a contagion they can ill afford." He looked pointedly at the boys.

She made no sound, though her eyes were wide with fear. She drew the boys closer, drawing the blankets tighter, covering her head as well.

Animals bawled and screamed, their hooves pounding as they tried to run. Kelubai was thankful he had brought his team of oxen in early or they would be lost with the others. He rose and edged near to the window, staying back while looking out. An acrid smell drifted in the cold air amid the pounding. The fields of flax that had just begun blooming were now in flames. Months of hard labor were going up in smoke.

"It's *Him*, isn't it?" Azubah said from her corner.

"Yes." It must be the same God who had turned the Nile to blood, brought on a plague of frogs, then gnats and flies, death to the livestock, and boils to all but the Hebrews in Goshen. "Yes. It's *Him*."

"You sound pleased."

"You have heard the stories I have. A deliverer will come."

"Not for us."

"Why not for us?"

"What are you saying, Kelubai?"

"Something my grandfather said to me when I was a boy." He came back and hunkered down before her and their sons. "A story passed down from our ancestor Jephunneh. He was a friend of Judah, the fourth son of Jacob, the patriarch of the twelve tribes." Kelubai remembered his grandfather's face in the firelight, grim, scoffing.

"I don't understand. We have nothing to do with the Hebrews."

He rose, pacing. "Not now. But back then, there was a connection. Judah's sons were half Canaanite. Two were said to have been struck down by this God. Shelah was the last one, named for Shelahphelah, the land in which he was born: Canaan. Two more sons were born to Judah by a woman named Tamar, also a Canaanite. And then he returned to his father's tents. This was during the time of the great famine. Everyone was starving, everywhere except here in Egypt. Then unbelievably, Judah's brother Joseph became overseer of Egypt and subject only to Pharaoh. Imagine. A slave becoming second only to Pharaoh. A great and mighty God had a hand in that!"

He looked out the window. "When the Hebrews arrived, they were welcomed and given the best land: Goshen. Jephunneh was descended from Esau, Judah's uncle, and he was a friend of Abdullam as well. So he gained the ear of Judah and made a pact in order to provide for our family. That's how we became slaves, theirs at first, farming land and growing crops so that the Hebrews were free to shepherd their growing flocks. It was a loathsome alliance, but necessary for survival. And then things turned around. Other rulers came. We were still slaves, but so were the Hebrews, and with each passing year, Pharaoh's heel bore down harder upon them than us."

"Why?"

He looked at her. "Who knows?"

Jealousy? Spite? More likely because they were fruitful and multiplied. One patriarch and twelve sons now numbered in the hundreds of thousands. There were as many Jews as there were stars in the heavens! Pharaoh probably feared if the Hebrews had wits and courage enough, they could rise up, join with Egypt's enemies, and gain their freedom. They could become masters over Egypt. Instead, they wailed and moaned as they worked, crying out to their unseen God to save them, and thereby making themselves the brunt of contempt and mockery.

Until now.

Kelubai looked up at the roiling dark sky in wonder. He could not see this God, but he was witnessing His power. The gods of Egypt were as nothing against Him. In the distance, the sun shone over Goshen. It would also seem this God could make a distinction between His people and the enemy. Pressing his lips together, Kelubai watched the fire sweep across the fields of barley. It had just come to head, harvest so close. Now, all lost.

There would be another famine after this night, and his family would suffer.

Unless . . .

A thin thread, a distant connection might be just enough to change everything.

Kelubai took a pellet from the sill. He rolled it between his fingers and popped it in his mouth. The stone was hard and cold against his tongue, but it melted warm and sweet, refreshing. His heart swelled at the sound and fury around him. He rejoiced in it. The God of the Hebrews could turn water to blood and call forth frogs, gnats, flies, and disease. Wind, water, fire, and air obeyed Him. Here was a God he could worship. Here was a God not carved by human hands!

Cupping his hands, he held them outstretched. His palms stung as the hard pellets struck, but he held his hands steady until a small pile had gathered. Then he tossed them back into his mouth and chewed the ice.

✦ ✦ ✦

Kelubai gathered his relatives. "If we are to survive, we must go to Goshen and live among the Jews."

"Live among the people Pharaoh despises? You're out of your mind, Kelubai!"

"The wheat and spelt are still growing. The gods of Egypt protected them. We still have those fields left."

Kelubai shook his head. "For how long?"

"The gods are at war, Kelubai. And we had best stay out of their way."

"What say you, Father?"

Hezron had been silent since the discussion began. Troubled, he raised his head. "It has been generations since our ancestor Jephunneh followed Judah from Canaan. The Hebrews will have long since forgotten how and why we came here."

"We will remind them we were once close friends of Judah."

"Close?" Kelubai's oldest brother, Jerahmeel, snorted. "A friend of a friend?"

"Father, did you not once say your father said his father's father took a Hebrew woman to wife?"

Ram was quick to follow their older brother's lead. "And how many years ago was that? Do you think the Hebrews will care that we have one of their women in our line? Ha! What use is a woman? What was the name of her father?"

Kelubai scowled. "Have you forgotten? The Hebrews came to us for straw when Pharaoh would not provide it."

"Straw we needed for our oxen."

Kelubai looked at Jerahmeel. "I gave all I had."

"Is that why you came to me for fodder for your animals?"

"Yes, it is. And now, if you but look around, you'll see there's nothing left for the animals to eat. Except in Goshen! There is pasturage there." Kelubai looked at his father. "And we have traded grain for goats. These are alliances we can build on."

"Alliances could bring the wrath of Pharaoh down upon us!" Jerahmeel stood, red-faced with impatient anger. "What protection will we have against his soldiers? No alliances. We must stay out of this war."

"Are you blind? Look around you, my brothers." Kelubai thrust his hand toward the barley and flax fields, flattened by hail, blackened by fire. "We're in the *middle* of the battlefield!"

"Pharaoh will prevail."

Kelubai gave a mirthless laugh. "Pharaoh and all his gods put together have not been able to protect Egypt from the God of the Hebrews. A river of blood, frogs, gnats, flies, boils! What will the God of the Hebrews send next?" He leaned forward. "We have heard the Hebrews wail for their deliverer. And their deliverer has come. Let us make Him ours as well."

"You mean Moses?"

"Moses is a man. He is but God's spokesman, telling Pharaoh what the God of the Hebrews has told him to say. It is an almighty God who destroyed our fields yesterday, and it is this God who will deliver His people."

"No." Jerahmeel glowered. "No, I say. *No!*"

Kelubai clung to self-control. Exploding in anger at his brother's stupidity would not convince their father to leave this place of desolation. He spread his hands and spoke more quietly. "What if we are left behind? What happens when Pharaoh and his officials are hungry and need grain? Will he say, 'My foolishness has brought destruction upon our land'? No, he won't. He'll send his soldiers to take whatever is left. The sacks of grain we have winnowed from our labors will be stolen from us. But we can take these stores with us to Goshen as gifts. All of the wheat and spelt."

"Gifts?"

"Yes, Ram. Gifts. We must align ourselves with the Jews. And we must do it now."

Kelubai felt his father's eyes upon him. He met that troubled stare with a look of fierce determination. "If we are to survive, Father, we must act *now!*"

His father looked at his other sons. "Perhaps Kelubai is right."

Flushed and angry, they protested, everyone talking at once. But no one had another solution to protect them from impending disaster.

"If Pharaoh hated the Hebrews before, he hates them all the more now."

"He'll be sending soldiers to Goshen again."

"Would you have the king of Egypt turn his hatred upon us as well?"

"Father, we had best stay out of this."

Kelubai had talked all morning and been unable to convince them. He would *not* waste any more time. He stood. "Do as you will, my brothers. Stay in your huts. Hope that whatever plague comes next will leave your barley untouched. As for me and my house, we'll be in Goshen before the sun sets, before another plague is upon us, a worse one than the last!"

His brothers all protested. "Better to wait and see what happens than be a headstrong fool."

Kelubai glared at his older brothers. "Wait long enough and you'll all be dead."

✦   ✦   ✦

By the time Kelubai returned to the land over which he had charge, Azubah had loaded the oxen with the plowshares, the pruning hooks, and the remaining sacks of grain from last year's harvest. Stacked on top were all the family possessions. Mesha would see to the small flock of goats that provided milk and meat.

Kelubai noticed a small wooden cabinet lashed to the side of the cart. "What's this?" he asked his wife, although he knew all too well.

"We can't leave our household gods behind."

He untied the box. "Have you learned nothing these past weeks?" Ignoring her shriek, he heaved the container against the wall of his empty hut. The cabinet burst open, spilling clay idols that smashed on the ground. He caught her by the arm before she could go after them. "They're useless, woman! Worse than useless." He took the rod from Mesha and prodded the oxen. "Now, let's go. We'll be fortunate if we reach Goshen before nightfall."

Others were heading for Goshen; even Egyptians were among those with their possessions on their backs or loaded in small carts. Squalid camps had sprung up like thistles around the outer edges of the humble Hebrew villages. Kelubai avoided them and went into the villages themselves, seeking information about the placement of the tribe of Judah. They camped away from everyone.

On the third day, he approached a gathering of old men in the middle of a village, knowing they would be the elders and leaders. Several noticed his approach and studied him nervously. "I am a friend come to join you."

"Friend? I don't know you." The elder glanced around the circle. "Do any of you know this man?" There was a rumble of voices as the others agreed that Kelubai was a stranger to all of them.

Kelubai came closer. "We are connected through my ancestor Jephunneh, friend of Judah, son of Jacob. Our people followed your family from Canaan during the great famine. We were your servants for a time."

"What is your name?"

"Kelubai."

"*Caleb*, he says." *Dog.* Some laughed, not pleasantly.

Kelubai felt the heat pour into his face. "Kelubai." He spoke slowly; his gaze went to each man in the circle in an unhurried clarification.

"Caleb," someone said again, snide and unseen.

And then another, "No doubt a friend of Egyptians."

Kelubai would not let insults or his temper rule his judgment. "I am your brother."

"A spy."

They seemed determine to insult him, these men who had been slaves all their lives.

Kelubai stepped inside the circle. "When the heel of
Pharaoh came down upon you, our family continued to
barter grain for goats. When Pharaoh denied you straw
to make bricks, I gave all I had. Do you so quickly forget
those who help you?"

"A little straw does not make you a brother."

These Hebrews were as hard to reason with as his own
family. Kelubai smiled mirthlessly. That alone should be a
sign that they were blood related. "I am a son of Abraham,
just as you are."

"A claim not yet established."

He faced the elder who spoke and inclined his head. "I
am descended from Abraham's grandson Esau, and Esau's
eldest son, Eliphaz."

Another snorted. "We have no commerce with Esau's
spawn."

"See how *red* his face is." *Edom.*

Kelubai's hackles rose. How did they come to be so
proud of Israel, the trickster, who cheated his brother,
Esau, out of his birthright! But he held his tongue, knowing it would not serve his purpose to argue that cause
before this council of men. Besides, Israel might have been
a deceiver, but Esau had been less than wise.

Someone laughed. "He has no answer to that!"

Kelubai turned his head slowly and stared into the
man's eyes. The laughter stopped.

"We are sons of Israel." The elder spoke quietly this
time, his words fact, not insult.

Did they think he would back down? "I am a son of
Abraham, who was called by God to leave his land and
go wherever God would take him."

"Is he speaking of Abraham or himself?"

"The dog thinks he is a lion."

Kelubai clenched his teeth. "As Abraham was called out of Ur, so too have we been called out of Egypt. Or do you think Moses speaks his own words and not the words of God?"

Kelubai might not be as pure in blood as they, but his desire to be counted among God's people went far beyond blood. It came from the very heart and soul of him. Could these men say the same, when they bowed down in worship one day and rose up in rebellion the next?

The old man assessed him. Kelubai felt a prickling of apprehension. Finally the elder held out his hand. "Sit. Tell us more."

Kelubai accepted the invitation. The others in the circle watched him closely, mouths tight, making it clear a hearing was not a vote of trust. He must choose his words carefully so he would not offend anyone. "You have good reason to be suspicious of strangers. Every time the Lord your God sends His prophet Moses to Pharaoh and another plague strikes Egypt, Pharaoh hates you all the more."

"We have had more trouble since Moses came out of the desert than we had before!"

Surprised, Kelubai glanced at the man who spoke. "What Moses says comes to pass. This is proof he is what he says he is—a messenger from God."

"He brings more trouble upon us!" the Israelite insisted.

Kelubai might as well be talking to his father and brothers. "Your animals survived the pestilence. Did any of you suffer boils? The hail and fire did not touch your lands. The God of Abraham is protecting you."

"And you want that protection for yourself. Isn't that the real reason you have come here and tried to worm your way into our tribe?"

"It is not *your* protection I seek." Clearly, some sitting in their council did not believe in the God who was fighting for their salvation. "You have as little power in yourself as I have." Kelubai drew a slow breath, and focused his attention on the elder who had invited him to sit. Here, at least, was a reasonable man. "I am a slave of Egypt. All my life I have worked for taskmasters, and all my life I have dreamed of freedom. And then I heard that the Nile had been turned to blood. I went to see for myself, and saw frogs as well—by the thousands—come up from the river into Thebes. Then gnats and flies by the millions! I saw oxen drop dead in harness because my neighbors did not heed the warning and bring the animals inside. Members of my family suffered from boils just as the Egyptians did. And a few days ago from the window of my hut, I watched the wheat fields in which I've toiled for months beaten down by stones of water and set aflame by spears of fire from heaven!"

At least they were silent now, all eyes on him, though some most unfriendly. "I *believe* Moses. Every plague that has come upon the land of Egypt weakens Pharaoh's power and brings us closer to freedom. The God who promised to deliver you has come, and He has shown He has the power to fulfill His Word!" He looked around the circle of elders. "I want—" he shook his head—"no. I *intend* to be counted among His people."

Some grumbled. "Intend? Such arrogance!"

"Honesty, not arrogance."

"Why bother to speak to the council at all?"

"I want to be shoulder to shoulder with you in whatever lies ahead, not nose to nose."

Others said what did it matter if this Edomite and his

family camped nearby? Hundreds of other people, Egyptians included, had put up tents around the village. What did one more man and his family matter as long as they brought their own provisions with them? Besides, wouldn't having such numbers around them afford a hedge of protection if Pharaoh sent his soldiers? They talked among themselves, argued, worried, fretted.

Kelubai sat and listened, measuring these men with whom he would be aligned. He had expected the Hebrews to be different. Instead, they reminded him of Jerahmeel and his younger brothers squabbling and carping, assuming and fearing the worst would happen. One would think they wished Moses had never been sent to Pharaoh to demand the slaves be released. One would think it would be better to go on making bricks for Pharaoh than risk even the hope of freedom!

Was it not a mighty God directing events that would open the way to salvation?

The old man, Zimri, watched Kelubai, his gaze enigmatic. Kelubai looked into his eyes and held his gaze, wanting the elder to know his thoughts. *I am here, Zimri. These men can ignore me, but neither they nor you will drive me away.*

It was hours later and nothing decided when the men began to disperse. God was ever on their lips, but clearly they did not trust the signs, nor the deliverer. When Kelubai rose, he saw Mesha waiting for him in the shadows between two huts. Smiling, he headed toward him.

"Caleb!"

Hackles rising, Kelubai turned and faced three men he knew to be his enemies. He remembered their names: Tobias, Jakim, and Nepheg. It was always wise to identify your enemies. Jakim raised his hand, pointing at him. "You don't belong among our people, let alone among the elders."

"I came to make a petition."

"Your petition has been rejected."

They spoke boldly now that the others were gone. "I will wait to hear what the entire council has to say." Not that it would make any difference. He was here to stay whether they liked it or not.

"We say, *Caleb*, stay outside the boundaries of our village if you know what's good for you. We don't want outsiders among us." They walked away.

"They called you a dog, Father!"

Yes, they had cast him among those wretched animals that lived on the outskirts of settlements, living off the scraps from the garbage heaps. He saw the shame in his son's eyes, anger flaring in his youthful confusion. More stinging was the unspoken question Kelubai saw in his son's eyes: *Why did you allow it?*

"They don't know me yet, my son."

"They insult you." Mesha's voice trembled with youthful fury.

"A man who gives in to anger might as well burn his house down over his head." He could swallow his pride when his family's survival was at stake.

Mesha hung his head, but not before Kelubai had seen the tears building. Did his son think him a coward? Time would have to teach the truth. "A wise man picks his battles carefully, my son." Kelubai put his arm around Mesha and turned him toward their camp on the outer edges of the village. "If they call me Caleb, so be it. I will make it a name of honor and courage."

✦   ✦   ✦

The family remained on the periphery of the villages of
Judah, but Kelubai stayed close whenever the council met
and therefore heard whatever news came at the same time
the Judeans did. And news did come by way of Levite
messengers from Moses and his brother, Aaron. Pharaoh
had hardened his heart again; another plague was coming.
It would not touch Goshen, but would lay waste to Egypt.

"We must go back and warn your father and brothers!"

Kelubai knew what his wife really wanted was to go
back, to be away from these Hebrews who would not
speak to her. "I warned them already. We will wait here
and make a place for them."

"What makes you so sure they'll come?"

"They aren't fools, Azubah. Stubborn, yes. Frightened?
As am I. No, we remain here. I left my words like seeds.
When they have been plowed under and more plagues
rain down upon them, what I said will take root and
grow."

The next morning, he went to the edge of Goshen and
watched the cloud of locusts come. They darkened the
sun. The noise was like a rumbling of chariots, like the
roar of a fire sweeping across the land, like a mighty army
moving into battle. The locusts marched like warriors,
never breaking ranks, never jostling each other. Each
moved according to the orders of the Commander, swarm-
ing over walls, entering houses through the windows. The
earth quaked as they advanced and the heavens trembled.
The ground undulated black. Every stalk of wheat and
spelt, every tree was consumed by the advancing horde
God had called into battle.

It won't be long now, Kelubai thought, watching the road for his father and brothers.

Kenaz came alone. "Jerahmeel rages against the god of the Hebrews for destroying the last of his crops."

"And Father?"

"You know Father cannot leave without his eldest son."

"And Jerahmeel will not come because it was *I* who suggested it. He is the fool!"

"You did not suggest, Kelubai. You commanded. Your manner did not sit well with our brothers." Kenaz smiled. "Since I am the youngest, it matters not what I think or whom I follow."

"You're wrong about that, my brother. You've shown courage by coming of your own free will, rather than bending to the will of those older and fiercer, but far less wise, than you." He looked toward the west. "If Pharaoh does not let the Hebrews go, there will be another plague, and another. Jerahmeel will change his mind."

✦   ✦   ✦

Trading and bartering for goatskins, Kelubai enlarged his tent enough to shelter his brothers and their families when they came.

Another plague did come, one of darkness upon the land of Egypt. But when Moses and Aaron returned to Goshen, they brought ill tidings of Pharaoh's fury. He would *not* allow the people to go with their flocks and herds, and he had threatened Moses that if Pharaoh ever saw him again, he'd kill him.

When Kelubai stood on the outer edge of the Jewish congregation and heard the instructions given by Moses' messenger, he knew the end was coming. He returned to

his camp and told Azubah he must go back and bring their
father to Goshen. "You must stay here with her, Kenaz,
and keep this camp secure. Now that the darkness has
lifted from Egypt, others will come seeking refuge among
the Hebrews. Hold our ground against them!"

Hastening to his father's house, he found his older
brothers had gathered their families. "Another plague is
coming!" Kelubai was thankful the locusts and darkness
had made them willing to listen. "I heard with my own
ears that all the firstborn sons will die in every family in
Egypt, from the oldest son of Pharaoh, who sits on the
throne, to the oldest son of his lowliest slave. Even the
firstborn of the animals will die."

Everyone looked at Jerahmeel, and he paled. Jerahmeel
looked at Kelubai with new respect. "You came back to
save my life?"

"We are brothers, are we not? But it is not only your
life I want spared, Jerahmeel, but those of your firstborn
son and the firstborn of all my brothers. Remember! *Every*
firstborn son."

Hezron stood. "We will return to Goshen with Kelubai.
Our animals are all dead. What little grain we had hidden
away for sustenance was eaten by locusts. There is nothing to hold us here."

They journeyed to Goshen willingly, setting up tents
close by Kelubai's camp. He called them together as soon
as they were settled. "Listen to what the Lord instructed
Moses. Each family is to sacrifice a year-old lamb or goat
without defect." The blood would be smeared over the
entrance to their tent, and they must remain inside until
death passed over them. The lamb or goat was to be
roasted with bitter herbs and eaten with bread made with-

out yeast. "We are to wear sandals, traveling clothes, and have walking sticks in our hands as we eat this meal."

When the night of the forewarned plague came, Kelubai, his wife and children, Kenaz, his father Hezron, and fourteen others stood around the fire pit as a goat roasted over the hot coals. Trembling in fear, they obeyed Moses' instructions exactly, hoping everyone inside the thin canopy would survive the night.

Kelubai heard a sound moving overhead, a whispering wind that made his blood run cold. He felt a dark presence press down upon them, press in from the thin leather flap that served as their door. All within the circle held their breath and pressed closer to one another. Kelubai shoved Mesha and Jerahmeel into the center of the family circle. "You die; we all die." Jerahmeel looked around, confused, shaken. When screams rent the cold night air, Azubah grasped Kelubai's robe and hid her face in its folds while their sons hugged close around him. A man screamed, and everyone in Kelubai's shelter jumped.

"We're all going to die!" Some began to weep.

"We won't die." Kelubai spoke with a confidence he was far from feeling. "Not if we put our faith in the unseen God."

Jerahmeel held his oldest son by the shoulders, keeping him close. "We've only goatskin to cover us, Kelubai, while the Hebrews have mud-brick huts and doors."

"Something is out there. . . ."

Fear grew in the room, fanned by more screams from outside. The children whimpered; the circle tightened.

"We must follow the instructions." Kelubai cut meat from the goat. He strove to keep his voice calm. "See to the bread, Azubah." She rose to obey.

"How can you expect us to eat at a time like this?"

"Because the God of Abraham demands it." Kelubai held out a slice of goat meat to his father. Hezron took it. "Give thanks to the God of Abraham for His protection from this plague of death."

Kelubai swallowed his fear and forced himself to eat the Passover meal. *Tomorrow will bring our freedom!*

✦   ✦   ✦

Egyptians came running toward Goshen, crying out, "Leave! Go quickly!"

"Pharaoh has relented!"

"Go as quickly as you can or all of us will die!"

"Hurry!"

"Here! Take this grain as a gift. Plead with your god for my life."

"Take my silver."

"Here is my gold!"

"Pray for us!"

"*Away with you! Hurry!*"

Others clutched at the Hebrews' robes, pleading, "Please, let us walk with you, for we've heard God is with you!"

Kelubai accepted the proffered gifts as his sons stripped down the goatskin coverings and yanked up the tent poles. He laughed. "Didn't I tell you all that our freedom was at hand?" Who would have imagined that God would make the Egyptians pour offerings upon them as they begged them to leave? Kelubai raised his hands in the air and shouted, "What a mighty God You are!" Laughing joyously, Kelubai heaved the last gift onto his cart. "Our taskmasters shower us with gifts and plead with us to leave!"

Azubah scrambled about, gathering their possessions and tying bundles while calling out to the children to keep the goats close. "Frogs, locusts, pestilence, and death! How do we worship such a God? No one gives without expecting to receive, Kelubai. What will this God ask of us?"

"So far He has asked nothing but that we believe what He says."

"And once we are in the wilderness, what will He ask of us then?"

"If He asked for everything, I would give it to Him."

"Our sons, Kelubai? Would you sacrifice our sons?"

Her fear gave him pause. The great overseers of Canaan were gods who thirsted for human blood. Was the God of Abraham such as these? If so, why had He asked for the blood of a lamb or goat rather than the blood of Israel's sons?

Kelubai prodded the ox, and caught up to his father and brothers who had set off before him. Having no animals or possessions to carry, they could travel faster than he.

Hezron shared his excitement, but Jerahmeel feared the future as much as Azubah. "And how many more will be out there in the desert waiting for us?"

"They will have heard what God has done for us."

"The nations may fear this God, but what reason have they to fear a band of slaves?"

Kelubai waved. "We are more than a band, brother. Look around you! We are thousands upon thousands."

"Scattered in a dozen tribes, with stragglers who cling like ticks. We are not a nation. We have no army."

"What need have we for an army when the God of heaven and earth fights for us? When people hear what has happened to Egypt, they will flee before us."

"Where do you come by this faith in a God whose people call you *dog*?"

Kelubai grinned coldly. "I've been called worse."

✦   ✦   ✦

The ragged mass traveled by day and night, moving south, away from the trade route. Deeper into the wilderness they moved before turning east, pressing between the high walls of a great wadi that spilled into the Red Sea. And there the masses huddled in family groups, crying out to Moses to save them when news came that Pharaoh and his army were not far behind them.

"Now see what you've done to us, Kelubai!" Jerahmeel ranted. "Had we stayed in Egypt our lives and the lives of our children would be safe."

Thousands screamed and wailed in terror when they realized they were blocked from all possible escape.

Kelubai lowered his head against the wind and pushed. "Stay in close with the Judeans." Wind whipped at his robe, stinging his face with sand and drops of salt water. "Stay together!" He hauled his wife and sons closer as a cloud caught flame. Raging overhead, it swirled into a pillar of fire that closed the wadi and stopped Pharaoh's chariots from racing out onto the spillway.

"They're moving!" Azubah cried out.

And so the multitude pressed forward as the sea opened before them clear to the other side, revealing the path of salvation. Some people ran down the slope. Others, burdened with possessions, moved slower. Kelubai shouted for Azubah to run ahead and take their sons with her while he followed with the oxen and cart. His father and brothers stayed with him, grabbing sacks to lighten the load and make the way swifter. Thousands came behind, pressing tight, moving down the road through the sea. When he reached high ground, Kelubai found his family waiting among the Judeans.

The pillar of fire had lifted, and Pharaoh's army raced out onto the sand and down into the pathway God had opened. Kelubai spotted Zimri among the stragglers. The old man, pale with exhaustion and sagging beneath the weight of a sack lumpy with possessions, struggled up the slope, his son, Carmi, helping him. Kelubai ran to them, grasped the pack, and supported the old man as they made their way up the hill.

"The chariots are coming," Kenaz shouted, reaching them and taking the pack. "They're coming! Hurry!"

A rushing sound and screams came from behind, and Kelubai felt a cold wet blast at his back. He fell forward onto his face and then felt hands upon him, dragging him up, shouting. Kelubai dug his heels into the wet ground and pushed, dragging Carmi up the slope. Lungs heaving, Kenaz flung the sack onto dry ground. Zimri was helped up, frightened but uninjured.

"They're gone." Kenaz stared out over the sea, searching. "All of them, gone."

The multitude was silent, staring out at the rippling sea as bodies of the Egyptian soldiers washed up along the shore.

Kelubai stood beside Zimri and Carmi. "Praise be to the God who saved us."

The old man was still pale, but he had regained his breath. He gripped Kelubai's arms for support. "My thanks, Caleb." For the first time, the term was spoken without derision. Caleb. *A new name for a new alliance. So be it.*

The old man's hands tightened. "Make your camp next to mine." His son, Carmi, grinned and slapped Caleb on the back.

✦   ✦   ✦

Before three days had passed, jubilation became complaining when the desert water was found to be bitter and undrinkable. Moses prayed and cast tree bark into the pond, enabling people to quench their thirst before traveling on to the date palms of Elim. Some would have been content to stay, but God had told Moses to lead His people into the wilderness. Why? was the common cry. Why didn't God lead them to green pastures and still waters instead of heading them out into an arid wasteland of sand and rock? Thirst and hunger soon set in, and the people complained for meat, as though God were a heavenly servant meant to give them whatever they craved. Moses prayed and God sent quail into the camp, so many that no one could walk without stepping on them. But in the morning, a greater miracle came when God gave them the bread of heaven to sustain them. Instructions were given to collect only enough for one day and no more.

Caleb knelt, picked up a few white flakes, and let them melt on his tongue. They were sweeter than anything he had ever tasted and held the slightest moisture of dew. When he had filled his clay jar, he rose and looked up at the cloud overshadowing the huge camp. It did not move with the air currents as other clouds did, nor disappear over the course of a hot day. It remained with the people, thick in portions, with fingers of gray-white, as though the mighty hand of God Himself shaded the Israelites and fellow travelers from the killing heat of the desert sun.

Freedom, water, food, shelter. Was there anything the
Lord had not given them?

Overwhelmed with emotions he could neither understand nor define, Caleb raised his omer high, tears streaming down his face. "How do I worship You, Lord? How do
I give thanks for my life? How am I to live from now on?
Nothing is the way I imagined it would be, oh, Lord!"

Life had become confusing. Freedom was not the sim-
ple matter he had dreamed. As a slave, he knew what the
day would hold and how to get through it. Now, he
didn't know what the next morning would bring. Every
day was different. He didn't know where he would camp
or for how long or why a particular place was chosen. He
pitched his tent near Zimri's each evening, but there
were always others around them, strangers vying for a
better position. How was he any different from all these
others, ambitious for themselves and their families, crav-
ing something better than what they had always known,
demanding more now that freedom had come and
brought with it the reality of daily decisions that had
always been made for them. Caleb had liked to think of
himself as more shrewd, more able to find his own way,
but realized now that he was the same as all the others.
He had been born and reared in a mud hut and lived all
his life on one small plot of land he worked for Pharaoh's
benefit. Now, he was in constant turmoil, out of his ele-
ment. Instead of dwelling in one place, he traveled great
distances and lived in a tent like a desert nomad. This
was not the life he had imagined.

Tense, irritable, fighting against the confusion of his
new life, fighting to keep his relatives together and in
some semblance of order, he felt more shame than joy. At

times, they behaved like a pack of wolves, growling at one another, fighting over scraps.

"Where are we going, brother? I thought we were supposed to be heading for Canaan, and we're in the middle of the wilderness!"

Every day had its squabbles and challenges. How did Moses hear the voice of God through the cacophony of voices raised in constant question and complaint?

Caleb struggled within himself, too.

In his heart, he cried out to God. *I don't want to question Your ways, Lord. I want to go with thanksgiving and without hesitation where You tell us to go. I want to set off into the unknown the way Moses does—head up, staff in hand. I don't want to look back with longing on the life I've known. Oh, God, help me to remember how unbearable it was and how I longed to be free. Is it possible for You to change a man? If so, change me!*

"Caleb!"

At the sound of Jerahmeel's annoyed voice, Caleb lowered the omer and held it against his chest, eyes closed, teeth clenched.

"We're on the move *again!* Though who but Moses can guess where we're going this time. As if there's a better place than this to rest . . ." Jerahmeel's complaining faded as he stalked away.

The cloud was moving now. In its changing shape, Caleb imagined its folds like an eagle with outspread wings, floating, head down watching them, not as prey but as sheltered offspring.

"*Caleb!* Are you going to just stand there? They're *moving!*"

And will You please change a few others as well?

+ + +

The people rose up in anger when they reached Rephidim, for there was no water. Caleb and his wife had given their water to their sons, and were as thirsty as everyone else. His relatives gave him no rest.

"It was your idea to follow this God. . . ."

"Where's the better life you promised?"

"I'm thirsty, Abba."

"How long before we get there?"

"Ask your abba where *there* is."

Caleb left them and sat among the rocks at the base of the high mountain. If he was going to die, he wanted to do it in peace and not surrounded by grumbling Israelites or relatives blaming him for every discomfort. Still, he heard the multitude crying out in the distance. Pressing his hands over his ears, he tried to shut out the angry shouting. His own wrath mounted, his heart pounding fast, his blood rushing hot and heavy.

How soon they all forget what You can do! You made the Nile run with blood. You brought forth plagues; You killed Egypt's livestock with pestilence. You covered the people with boils, destroyed the land with hail and fire, and killed the firstborn from Pharaoh on down, all the while sparing the animals and lives of those who belong to You. And still that madman Pharaoh changed his mind and came after us!

But You opened the sea, made a dry pathway across, then closed it again over Pharaoh's army, washing them away like dust before a windstorm. The sea. The Nile. The river of life . . . no. No! Who but a fool would long for that place of slavery and death?

Water, Lord. Please. Water is a small thing, but we will

die without it. Oh, hear us, God who commands the heavens and the earth. Help us!

Tongue parched, throat closing, his skin so dry he felt his body shrinking, he closed his eyes. If not for the cloud overhead, Caleb knew he would have perished already, baked in the heat, dried out like a Nile fish on a rack.

Why am I still alive? What is the purpose in all this suffering? I don't understand You. Did You set us free only to allow us to die of thirst? It makes no sense. Water, Lord. Oh, God of might and mercy, please, give us water. I don't believe You brought us out here to die. I don't believe it. I won't believe it!

The cries of the mob suddenly changed to screams of excitement and exultation. Trembling from weakness, Caleb stood and took a few steps so he could see what was happening. Water gushed from a rock in the side of the mountain, forming a stream that raced down and pooled. Thousands sank to their knees and fell forward onto their hands to thrust their faces into the water and drink like animals. Another miracle! Another, just when they needed it most.

Stumbling, Caleb made his way down the rocky slope. Pressing his way through the celebrants, his gaze never leaving the rock that flowed water, he squatted, cupped his hands, and drank. The Rock itself was the well of life-giving water. The stream flowed straight from the stone, fresh and clear and cool. As Caleb drank deeply, he felt his body renewed, strengthened, revitalized. Closing his eyes, he held the precious water and washed his face, longing to immerse himself in it.

As the people were quenching their thirst, Caleb heard shouting.

"The Amalekites are attacking! They are killing the stragglers!"

Moses called for Joshua. People cried out again, frightened this time.

"They'll soon be upon us!"

"We have no army to fight against the Amalekites!"

Caleb rose, dripping, and ran to his camp. He rummaged through the possessions he had brought from Egypt until he found his scythe. "Come on." He raised his farm implement and called to his brothers. "Fight for our brothers!"

"We're not soldiers." Jerahmeel stood back. "We're farmers."

Caleb faced him, angry. "Should not a farmer fight for his neighbors?"

"Who is my neighbor?"

There was no time to stand and argue. People were dying! Turning his back on his father and brothers, Caleb ran after Joshua. Others had gathered with Moses' young servant. Moses had already given instructions and now climbed the mountain, his brother, Aaron, on one side and his friend Hur on the other.

Caleb peered through the crowd to the man in its center. Joshua looked so young and nervous. The men around him were tense, shifting, uncertain. Caleb felt uneasy. What did he know about fighting against a trained enemy?

He remembered what God had done for them already. The Lord, He would protect them. The Lord, He would give them victory. *I will believe that. I will set my mind upon Him. I will proclaim my faith before these men loud enough that they will all hear and know I am for the Lord!*

"Let me through!" Lowering his head, Caleb shoved his way through the crowd until he stood before Joshua. "We are God's to command, Joshua. And the Lord has designated you to lead." Caleb looked around and raised his voice. "God will fight for us! He did not bring us out into this desert to be picked off by cowardly marauders who kill the weak and helpless, nor by any who bow down to false gods!" Baring his teeth in a grin, Caleb stared Joshua in the eye. "Command us as God commands you. The battle is the Lord's!"

Joshua's eyes shone with sudden fierceness. He let out a shout and the others joined with him.

And so they went out into battle armed with farm implements and threshing tools, while three old men stood on the mountain praying.

And God gave them victory.

After the triumph came the lingering stillness. Caleb waited along with thousands of others camped at the base of the mountain while Moses went up to meet with the Lord. Days passed, and long nights of quiet and question.

Waiting proved a greater test than taking up arms against the enemy.

CALEB sat in misery, staring up at the mountain. *Here I sit, coward that I am, an outsider again.* He hung his head.

Washed, adorned in clean garments, consecrated, he had stood with the multitude, eager to hear the Lord. He had heard God blow the shofar blast. The sound of it, long and heavy, had rattled his chest. A consuming fire had flared from the mountaintop, along with a thunderous roar. He had fled in terror. Like stampeding sheep, thousands had run. And like the others, he had cowered at a distance. Let Moses listen to God and tell them what He said.

Moses was on the mountain again, but this time he had taken the elders with him, including Zimri from the tribe of Judah. Joshua, too, had been summoned.

Mortified by his own cowardice, Caleb spoke to no one. He knew he had missed his chance to be close to God. Covering his face, he wept.

When Aaron and the elders returned, Caleb went to hear what Zimri had to tell the sons of Judah.

"We saw the God of Israel; under His feet there was a pavement of sapphire, as clear as the sky itself." Zimri shook with excitement, his eyes shining. "And He did not stretch out His hand against us. We ate and drank in praise of Him. And then the Lord called Moses up the mountain. God will give him the laws we are to live by."

"Where is Joshua? What happened to him?"

"Joshua went up the mountain with Moses. We could see them both as they went up. Then they stopped and waited for six days. On the seventh, the mountain caught

fire and Moses went into the cloud and disappeared.
Joshua is still up there waiting for him."

"Are Moses and Joshua alive?"

"God only knows."

"Before Moses went up, he told us to wait, and we did
wait."

"Did they take anything up with them? Food? Water?"

"Nothing."

Days passed, then weeks. The people grew restless.
Moses was surely dead. Why were they still camped in
this desolate place? Why didn't they return to Egypt?
They need not fear going back now. Surely, after all the
plagues, the Egyptians would be in fear of them?

"Why should they fear us?" Caleb remonstrated with
his family. "*We* did not bring the plagues. *God* did!"

"We should get out of here before he decides to kill us
the way he's killed Moses."

"We don't know that Moses is dead."

Jerahmeel stood. "He's been gone a month, Caleb!
He's an old man, and he went up that mountain without
food and water. What do you think has happened to
him?"

"He lived in Midian forty years before he returned to
Egypt. That old man knows how to survive in the desert."

Hezron stood between them. "Kelubai, you were right
in leading us to Goshen. We are free from slavery. But
now, it is time to go back to Egypt or go on to Canaan. We
cannot stay here forever."

Caleb clenched his hands. "Why not? We have water.
We have manna."

"What sort of a life is this?" Jerahmeel raged. "I'm sick
of manna. The sweetness of it sticks in my throat."

"In Egypt, you never knew from one day to the next if you would have bread to eat!"

Jerahmeel turned to the others. "We should go back to Egypt. They fear us. Even the gods fear us. We can fashion gods and show that we have returned as brothers."

Caleb sneered. "Return to gods who had no power to protect themselves?"

"And what good is this god doing for us now? We sit and wait. Weeks we have waited. Are we to live the rest of our lives at the base of this mountain?"

"Go then, and see how far you get without His protection."

"We won't be going alone, Caleb. Everywhere I turn, others are saying the same thing I am saying. Even that old man you follow around, Zimri, has gone with others to speak to Aaron."

"And what does Aaron say?"

"At first he said to wait. Now he says nothing."

Caleb went outside. He couldn't abide the air inside the tent any longer. He looked up at the mountain. Nothing had changed. The cloud remained, surges of light flashing from within. Why would God kill Moses? What sense did that make? And yet, if the old man hadn't died, why did he linger up there? And where was Joshua?

He clenched his fist. "I will not believe You brought us out here only to abandon us. I won't believe it."

"Kelubai?"

Azubah stood at the doorway. She came to him hesitantly, her gaze troubled. "Why are you so determined to believe in this God?"

"What is the alternative?"

"Return to Egypt."

"Yes, and I would rather my sons die here than go back to that place of death."

"It will be different this time, Kelubai."

"Woman, you speak of things you do not understand."

Her chin jutted. "Ah, yes, as you understand this God. As you understand why we must remain here, day after day, waiting for no one knows what."

"You would do better to listen to me rather than my brother."

"I listen to you, but you would do better to listen to your father." She went back into the tent.

Frustrated, Caleb walked away into the night. How he longed to climb that mountain and find out for himself what had happened to Moses. But there was a boundary set; the mountain was sacred ground. He would not set foot upon it.

Wandering among the clustered camps, Caleb heard others talking. Jerahmeel had spoken the truth. He was not the only man counseling a return to Egypt. It was near dawn when he returned to his tent, exhausted and disheartened, and went to bed.

Azubah awakened him. "Messengers came through camp, my husband. Aaron has called for the men to bring him a pair of gold earrings from each wife, son, and daughter." She had already collected the earrings in a cloth.

"What for?"

"Does it matter? Your father and brothers wait outside."

"Hurry!" Jerahmeel appeared at the entrance to the tent. "Baskets are set outside Aaron's tent, and they are overflowing with gold earrings. Some put in necklaces and bracelets."

"Give whatever you want." Angry, Caleb turned over on his pallet. He was too tired and despondent to care why Aaron had asked for gold.

He found out soon enough. Word spread. All were to come and worship before the Lord. Caleb went eagerly, his family with him. Shocked, he found himself standing before a golden calf much like those he had seen in Egypt. This one was far from the svelte beasts set upon pedestals in Egypt. "Where did it come from?"

"Aaron made it for us."

"Aaron?" He couldn't believe Moses' brother would make such a thing. But there he was, standing before the gathering, presiding over it, calling for offerings to the God who had brought them out of Egypt.

This cannot be! Confused, Caleb drew back.

The people bowed down and presented offerings. Azubah and Caleb's sons, his brothers and father went forward. No one trembled and shook before this god. Instead, they rose up to laugh and dance and celebrate. Aaron proclaimed a feast. Caleb didn't know what to do. Sick and confused, he returned to his tent.

Music filled the camp. Then shrieking and laughter. Azubah came in and lay down beside him, her eyes dark. She smelled of incense and tasted of wine. "This is better, isn't it?" She moved over him, wanton, eager.

Caleb caught his breath. Maybe it was better not to think about a God he couldn't understand. But, somehow, this didn't feel right. He wanted to push her away, but she kissed him. His senses swam. She was his wife, after all. Surely, there was nothing wrong in this. Maybe it was better not to trouble himself with inexplicable feelings of shame and guilt. "Azubah . . ."

"Love me."

Why should he feel guilty? Maybe it was better to live
and not think at all. *God, God.* No. He would not think of
God right now. Not now. Grasping Azubah's flowing hair,
he took what she offered, surrendering himself to the fire
in his belly. Passion rose, crested, and evaporated, leaving
in its wake a sense of shame and bewilderment. Caleb lay
in the darkness, with Azubah, sated, asleep beside him.
Never had he felt so unclean.

The camp was in an uproar. "What's going on now?"
His wife slept on, the effects of the wine deadening her to
sound and light. She would have a headache when she
awakened. Caleb dressed and went outside.

Moses had returned! He strode through the camp,
shouting.

"He destroyed the stone tablets!"

Caleb caught hold of a man running away. "What stone
tablets?"

"The ones on which God wrote the laws we were to follow!"

Caleb ran toward the screaming. Moses climbed onto
the platform and pushed the calf off its stand. "Burn it."
His face was red, his eyes filled with wrath. "Grind it into
powder. Spread it over the drinking water."

The people were out of control, some drunk and unwilling to give up their pleasure taking, others screaming defiance.

Caleb felt the gathering storm. Aaron was running. He
shouted, and others from his tribe of Levi raced to stand
behind Moses. Some had swords and drew them.

With sudden understanding, Caleb cried out. He saw
his sons among the crowd gathering against Moses.

"Mesha! Mareshah! Jesher! Come out from among those people. Shobab! Ardon! Come to me. Hurry!" His sons wove their way through the crowd, eyes wide. He ran to meet them, grabbed them, and dove to the ground. When they cried out in panic and tried to rise and run, he yanked them down. "Bow down before the Lord. Bow down!"

Screams of rage and death came all around him. Someone stepped over him. Metal struck metal, words exchanged, a gurgling cry, a thud. His heart pounded. Reason kept him on his face. "Forgive us, Lord. Forgive us. God, forgive us."

If this was Moses' fury vented, what could God in His wrath do?

When a man fell dead beside them, Ardon screamed and tried to rise. Caleb yanked him down again, sliding half over him to hold him to the ground. "Mercy, Lord! Mercy!" His sons sobbed in terror. "Pray for forgiveness! Pray!" Caleb ordered them.

"God, forgive us . . ."

"God, forgive . . ."

Would the Lord hear such soft cries amidst the chaos of terror surging all around them?

The battle was soon over. Sobs and wailing rose.

Jerahmeel lay dead near his tent. So, too, another brother. Their wives lay dead nearby. Hezron sat at the opening of his tent, rocking back and forth, face ashen, his garments torn in grieving. When Azubah came outside, bleary-eyed, and saw what had happened, she wailed and threw dust into the air. Silent, Caleb commanded his sons to help him carry the bodies outside the camp for burial.

Would his family blame him for the deaths? Would they cry out against him because he had fought so hard to come with the Israelites and follow after their God? Would they want to turn back now?

When he returned to his tent, he found everyone silent. No one looked at him, not even his wife and sons. "You blame me for their deaths, don't you?"

"We should have turned back when we had the chance."

"Turned back to what, Father? Slavery?"

"*My sons are dead!*"

My brothers, Caleb wanted to add, but he hunkered down and spoke gently. "We must give honor only to the God who delivered us."

"Should we not have choice in which god we worship?"

He looked at Azubah. "Will my own wife turn against me? Not one, not *all* of the gods of Egypt could stand against the Lord God of Israel." She disgusted him. He disgusted himself.

"Aaron made the golden calf and Aaron still lives."

"Yes, Father, because he ran to Moses when asked where he stood. Had my brothers bowed down before the Lord, they would still be alive. But instead, they chose to defy God and Moses. They chose death over life."

The old man sobbed.

Mourning deeply, Caleb removed his jewelry. As he lifted an amulet from his neck, he looked at it and went cold. Why had he not noticed it was the Star of Rompha? He wore the cobra Ra on his arm, a lapis scarab set in solid gold on his finger. Shuddering, he yanked off every piece of jewelry he wore. "Take off everything that honors another god." They did as he said, casting off gifts the Egyptians had poured upon them. "It's a wonder we aren't all dead!"

+ + +

Moses had chiseled out two more stone tablets and gone back up the mountain to plead with God on the people's behalf. When he returned, his face shone like the sun. Until he covered his face with a veil, no one had courage enough to go near him, not even his brother, Aaron. Moses had not returned empty-handed; he brought back the Law written by God's hand upon the tablets, and plans for a tabernacle and holy items including an ark to contain the Law. God had chosen two men for the task of building the Tabernacle: Bezalel and Oholiab. Offerings were needed for the construction, and the people responded. Had not God provided what was needed by the gifts the Egyptians had given the Israelites? The people merely gave back a portion of what God had already given them.

Caleb gave the best of what he had.

"Enough!" Moses' servants said. "We have enough!"

Everyone worked. Even Azubah. She joined other women of the family and wove fine cloth. Caleb's remaining brothers helped keep the fires burning so the gold and bronze could be melted. Caleb worked hard, honored to be assigned any task alongside the sons of Judah. But he knew alliances weakened under stress. He had to find another way to be grafted in among these people.

Young women wore mourning clothes. Many had lost fathers and brothers on the day of God's retribution for the golden idol. Caleb saw in them a way to solidify his family's connection to the tribe of Judah.

He approached his father and brothers. "We must strengthen our alliance with Judah."

"How?" Kenaz spoke with willingness.

"Take wives from among the sons of Judah."

Caleb took a second wife, Jerioth. His father and Kenaz followed his lead, as did the others over the next months.

Each morning, Caleb listened eagerly to the laws God had given Moses. He wanted to please the God of heaven and earth. Though the task of following the numerous laws was daunting, he felt hedged in from all sides, safe under the watchful eye of God.

Know my heart, Lord. Know that I desire to please You.

When the Tabernacle and holy items were ready, Caleb stood amidst the multitude, shoulder to shoulder for the dedication ceremonies, praying that God would be pleased with their work. He did not hold a place in the front, so he had to stretch up to see, and strain to hear what was said. Giving up, he kept his gaze fixed upon the cloud. When it moved, his heart fluttered and then pounded. In awe, he drew in his breath and held it. When the cloud came down and filled the tabernacle, there was weeping in joy. Caleb shouted praise to God.

The joy was short-lived.

"Aaron's sons are dead!" People shouted and wept. Some ran.

"What happened?"

"They were consumed by fire!"

"Why?"

Caleb heard later that they had scorned the law of the Lord and offered incense in a manner other than that which God commanded. Fear gripped Caleb. If God would kill Aaron's sons, He would not tolerate sin among any of

His people. Caleb was afraid to turn to the left or right of what the Lord commanded.

Zimri represented Judah among the seventy elders instructing the sons of Judah. Whenever the old man sat to teach the laws Moses had received from the Lord, Caleb was there, listening more intently than the younger men who gathered.

As the people moved toward the Promised Land, more trouble brewed. The Egyptian rabble traveling with them complained about the manna. They longed for the fish, cucumber, melons, leeks, onions, and garlic of their homeland. "We are sick of nothing at all to eat except this manna!" The Israelites took up the rebellious whining. Even the sons of Judah began complaining.

"These people have learned nothing." Caleb kept his wives and sons inside the tent. "Do they think the Lord does not hear their carping?"

Jerioth said nothing, but Azubah argued. "I am as sick of the manna as they are. I can barely swallow it without gagging on the sweetness of it."

"You try my patience, woman. When will you learn to give thanks for what God has given us?"

"I am thankful, but must we have the same thing day after day?"

"You lived on barley cakes and water in Egypt and never once complained."

"Yes, but this God could give us anything and everything we want. Why does He withhold a *feast* from heaven and instead make us grovel on our knees every morning for one day's portion of manna? I'm sick of it— sick of it, I say. I wish we had never left Egypt!"

Then God sent quail and a plague.

Azubah feasted on roasted birds and died.

Remembering her as a young bride and mother, Caleb grieved. Leaving Jerioth in camp to tend the baby, he and his other sons carried Azubah's body outside the camp. They buried her among thousands of others. Weeping, Caleb went down on his knees and stretched out his hands, his gaze fixed upon the cloud. *Why won't they listen, Lord? How is it I believe and so many don't? They saw the plagues of Egypt. They walked through the sea. They saw the water come from the rock. They've eaten the manna. Why, Lord? Why won't they believe?*

Thirty days after Azubah's death, Caleb sought another wife from among the daughters of Judah left fatherless.

Zimri advised him. "Ephrathah would be a good choice."

The Hebrews overhearing the conversation exchanged smiles, and Caleb suspected that no one else wanted the woman. So be it. He would do whatever necessary to solidify his family's alliance with Zimri, even if it meant taking some loathsome woman off his hands.

"I will make arrangements for the bride-price."

Several men laughed low and bent their heads close to whisper. Zimri gripped Caleb's arm. "Do not take heed of those who only take notice of the surface."

Ephrathah was brought to his tent. When Caleb lifted her veil, his suspicions were confirmed. He treated her with consideration if not affection.

✦   ✦   ✦

Another rebellion arose, this time between the high priest, Aaron, and Miriam over Moses' Cushite wife. The Lord struck Miriam with leprosy and then healed her when Aaron pleaded for her. Even so, the law required Miriam to spend seven days outside the camp. Everyone waited for her return, for she was held in high esteem as the sister of Moses, the one who had watched over him as he drifted on the Nile and then been bold enough to speak to Pharaoh's daughter about his need for a wet nurse. The cunning girl had brought back their mother to tend him.

+　　+　　+

Caleb loved to listen to Ephrathah's stories. She knew the history of her people in a way he had never heard it. She was more eloquent than Zimri and the elders! Every bit of information he could gather helped him pry into the boundaries of his adopted tribe. He smiled as his sons leaned in close, listening hungrily. This new wife of his had the gift of storytelling. Seeing her more clearly, he cherished her. Ephrathah was as stubborn in her faith as he. Even Jerioth, about to bear her second child, deferred to Ephrathah.

"Moses drifted among the crocodiles and serpents." Ephrathah moved her hands sinuously as she told the story of Moses. "Even the wise ibises paid no attention. Israel's deliverer was within their reach, and they did not know. And where did the Lord take the babe, but straight into the arms of the daughter of His enemy, Pharaoh. Moses' sister, Miriam, came out of hiding then and said the baby needed a wet nurse and would the lady like her to fetch one. Of course, she did, having no milk to offer. And so it was that Jochebed, Moses' own mother, received her son back again." Ephrathah laughed. "The Lord laughs at His enemies, for they have no power against Him."

Caleb drew Ephrathah close in his arms that night. He whispered into the curve of her neck, "You are worth your weight in gold."

✦   ✦   ✦

Zimri and the other elders of Judah called the heads of families together. Moses had called for twelve spies to enter Canaan, one from each tribe. Judah must choose a representative.

Dozens of men volunteered, Caleb among them. Though he quaked at the thought of entering Canaan without the Lord overhead, he knew if he was chosen, he and his family would hold a place of honor from this time forward. "Let me. I'm not afraid. Send me!"

Everyone started talking at once and no one heard him but those standing close. They sneered. The elders were calling for discussion.

"It should be a young man without wife and children on such a journey."

"There is no guarantee the man will return alive."

"There are giants in the land. Descendants of Anak."

At that, some men changed their minds about volunteering.

Voices grew louder. "Let each family offer one, and we will cast lots to see who the Lord will send."

If that happened, Caleb knew he stood no chance. He shoved into the circle. "I will go." His sons would have a place among God's people even if he had to sacrifice his life to make certain of it.

The gathering fell silent. Several looked to Zimri.

The old man shook his head. "No."

Caleb faced the old man he had saved. "Why not?" He

looked around the circle. "I don't see all that many jump-
ing at the chance to go."

"You have two wives and sons."

"Not to mention the rabble who came with him!"
another called out from the back.

Caleb seethed, but forced himself to offer a wry smile.
"Why not send the dog if he's so eager to sniff out
Canaan?" Some laughed at Caleb's challenge. Others
called out agreement. "What do you say? Will you send
the Caleb?" A cry of agreement rose amidst the laughter.
Caleb laughed loudest, determined. "Mock me if you
will, but send me. If I die in Canaan, what have you
lost?"

"Nothing!"

"Enough!" Zimri shouted. "Hear me." The men grew
quiet. "Moses has called for men who are leaders. He is no
leader who mocks his brother." Caleb felt the heat surge
into his face and then realized Zimri's scowl was directed
at the man who had started the baiting. The offender lowered his gaze. Zimri looked at the others. "Who will represent Judah on this perilous errand? Step forward if you're
willing. Otherwise, be silent."

Emboldened by Zimri's defense, Caleb stepped into the
center of the circle. "Send me."

"You are not equipped."

"Did I not go into battle beside Joshua against the
Amalekites?"

"You are my friend, Caleb, but you are not . . ."

"Full-blooded." Another man finished what Zimri was
too kind to voice.

Caleb's face flushed hot as he looked between the
elders. "Did I not hear you just call me brother?"

"We have an alliance with you, but it must be a Judean by birth that should go on our behalf."

That these words should come from Zimri hurt deeply, for he had thought him an ally. "And where is he?" Caleb swept his hand toward those standing silent.

Zimri frowned. "You are not a young man, Caleb."

"I am forty years old, and I come with forty years of life experience." He turned his back on Zimri and walked the circle, pausing to look into the face of each man he passed. "Do you want to go? Do you? Come on! Step forward if you're willing to face the Anak." No one held his gaze for long. "The man who goes into Canaan will not just be looking at the enemy we must fight, at their city walls and weapons, but at the land itself. Should Judah not have the best? All of you here were brick makers and shepherds. I was a farmer. I made my living off the land. To have good crops, you need good land. I offer myself as your servant. *Send me.*"

Everyone started talking at once again.

"Let God decide," someone called out, and others joined in.

Zimri and the elders commanded order again and called for a lottery. "One man from each family must bring a lot. We will let the Lord decide."

And there was an end to further discussion. Grim and despairing, Caleb had his name etched upon a bone and tossed it into the growing pile. The census had counted 74,600 men twenty years and older in the tribe of Judah. There would be thousands of lots cast before the choice was known. The lots were shaken and cast and the elimination process began. It would take the rest of the night, if not longer.

Ephrathah tried to soothe him, but Caleb went off by himself and sat looking up at the pillar of fire swirling in the night sky. He spread his hands, palms up. He had no words to express his longing. *I am as afraid as any man to go into Canaan and walk among the giants who live there. But I fear more not being counted among Your people. Do not allow them to set me aside. Please don't reject me, Lord. Purify my blood. Make me a son of Israel!*

He covered his head. "I know I am not fully Hebrew, Lord. I know Esau's blood runs in my veins. But even so, Lord . . ." He lifted his head, tears streaming down his cheeks. "You are my God. You and only You. There is no other."

He knew there were many who disliked him, who thought he was proud and ambitious, a thorn in their sides. Some wished he would turn around and go back to Egypt. They saw him as a growling, groveling dog on the edge of the camp. And didn't he behave like one, barking constantly for what he wanted? A place among God's people! He groaned. Who was he to think himself worthy to represent the tribe of Judah? Surely the Lord looked down and saw him for the cur he was. He hunched against the rock, too depressed to go back to camp.

Dawn came and went. It was midday before he returned to his tent.

Zimri was there in the shady entrance of Caleb's tent, sipping a drink Ephrathah had just replenished.

Caleb sat with him. "I'm sorry I put you in an awkward position, Zimri. I had no right to demand that I be chosen to represent Judah. I'm not worthy."

The old man opened his hand. Caleb's lot lay on his palm.

He took the lot and turned it over and over in his hand. "You removed it from the pile."

"I did."

Caleb felt as though he had been kicked in the gut. It was a moment before he could speak. "I thought being counted in the census at least gave me the right to take part in the lottery."

"You misunderstand me, Caleb."

"So it would seem." Caleb looked out at the other tents clustered close. He did not want Zimri to see his deep hurt. Angry words rose, but he held them back. Rash speaking would cause a permanent rift between them, and Caleb had few friends among the sons of Judah as it was. "Who won the lottery?"

"You are the only man I know who would see it as winning."

Caleb gave a bleak laugh. "Who is God sending?"

"Who do you think?" The old man stared at him. After a moment, he smiled faintly. "It would seem among all the men of Judah, God has chosen you to represent us."

Caleb felt gooseflesh rise up and down his back and arms. First joy, then terror, filled him. He released his breath unevenly.

Zimri laughed. "Wonders never cease, my friend. This is the first time I've seen you speechless." He rose. "Report to Moses and he will give you further instructions. Whatever you need, Caleb, anything, you have only to ask. The men of Judah will give it."

+ + +

When Caleb saw Joshua among the other spies, he pressed his way through the men gathered. "Ah, my young friend." Caleb grinned. "Let an old man travel with you. Between us, we will have the impetuousness of youth and the cunning of age on our side."

Joshua laughed. "I wondered if Judah would send you."

They clasped hands. "God sent me."

"I would meet your friend, Joshua."

Caleb would know that voice if it had spoken to him in darkness. Heart hammering, he turned and bowed his head low to Moses. He had never been this close to God's chosen prophet. Aaron, dressed in the garments of high priest, stood behind his brother, forgiven and restored by God.

"Do not bow low before me." Moses put his hand upon Caleb. "I am but a man."

Caleb straightened. "A man, yes, but God's anointed prophet who speaks the Word of the Lord. You have pleaded for our lives when we deserved death. And God granted us mercy. May the Lord grant you long life and teach us obedience."

Joshua grasped his shoulder. "This is Caleb of the tribe of Judah."

"Ah, yes. I saw you fight alongside Joshua against the Amalekites."

Stunned that he had been noticed, Caleb received his blessing.

Moses gathered the men. "The Lord told me to send out from the people men to explore the land of Canaan, which He is going to give to us. Go northward through the Negev into the hill country. See what the land is like and find out whether the people living there are strong or weak, few or many. What kind of land do they live in?

Is it good or bad? Do their towns have walls or are they unprotected? How is the soil? Is it fertile or poor? Are there many trees? Enter the land boldly, and bring back samples of the crops you see."

After praying for them and blessing them, Moses and Aaron left them alone to make their plans for departure.

The men agreed to meet at dawn and leave together.

Caleb, with ideas of his own, returned to his tent to make preparations.

When he arrived at the agreed meeting site the next morning, the others stared and spoke in derision. "You look like an Egyptian trader."

Caleb grinned. "Good." Dressed in finery, he held the lead rope of three donkeys laden with trade goods donated by the men of Judah, and another with a saddle, but no rider. "This is the best way to get inside the walled cities and take a good look around."

"*Inside* the walls? Are you out of your mind?"

"We can see all we need to see from the outside."

It was too early to argue. "You go your way, and we will go ours." He tossed the reins to Joshua, then tapped the flank of his mount with a stick and set off. Once away from Kadesh and the multitude and camped the first night on their own in the wilderness of Paran, he would be able to speak with these men. Perhaps then they would listen. The others came along behind, mumbling.

Joshua rode alongside him. "What do you have in mind?" He did not look comfortable mounted.

Caleb swung his leg off the donkey. Joshua dismounted and they walked together. "Here is how I see it, Joshua. We need to find out everything we can about Canaanite defenses, and you can't do that by skirting around a city.

You have to go inside and see what war machines they have, if any, how strong their walls are, where the weak points exist."

"How does a farmer come to know anything about warfare?"

"I don't know much, my friend, but I have learned to observe everything around me. We listen to the wind and watch the movement of the stars and passing of seasons. I think there may be more than one reason for each command the Lord gives us."

Joshua tilted his head. "Go on."

"We know God fights for us. He destroyed Egypt with the plagues and opened a sea to give us safe passage out of Egypt. We know He has promised to give us Canaan. But we continue to test Him. It seems part of our nature to rebel against the Lord. Who knows what tomorrow may bring, Joshua. But there may be more than one reason why God sends us to view the land and people." Caleb smiled bleakly. "If we fail again, what will God have us do?" Or what would God do to them?

"We won't fail."

"I have faith in God, my friend, but little faith in men."

They camped on the desolate southern edge of the wilderness of Zin. When they reached the dry mountain terrain of the Negev, Caleb thought it wise to split into smaller groups.

"We're safer together."

"Two men can move more quickly than twelve, and six groups will see more of Canaan than one."

"There is that to consider." Joshua's face shone bronze in the firelight. "And another. If we come as one, we will draw attention to ourselves, and the Canaanites may view us as a threat. If we travel in pairs, we can melt in, mingle. Take note of everything you see. Join others traveling and listen. We will meet here and make the journey back together."

Caleb had another idea. "Wherever you go, speak of what happened in Egypt. Spread the news that the Lord God of Israel overcame the gods of Egypt and delivered the Hebrews from slavery."

The others spoke in protest. "We may be questioned by leaders if we do that."

"The less we talk about what God did to Egypt the safer for us."

Even Joshua looked troubled by Caleb's suggestion. Caleb tried to reason with them. "God called for leaders from among the tribes of Israel. Men of courage! You are all younger than me, but where is the fire of youth? Didn't you hear what Moses said? The Lord has given us the land already. Canaan is already ours. We are being sent merely to see and report to the people the great gift God has given us."

"Do you really think we'll just stroll into Canaan and the inhabitants will flee before us?"

"If they know the God who is with us, yes! With the Lord on our side, who will dare come against us? Let the Canaanites know what has befallen Egypt so that the fear of the Lord will fall upon them. Then they will run from us when Moses leads us into Canaan."

Shaphat of Simeon stood. "A bold plan, Caleb."

Shammua of Reuben shook his head. "A little too bold, in my opinion."

"Should we not be bold? Look to the Lord who . . ."

"Look things over!" Palti of Benjamin said. "That's what Moses said. That's all he said."

They ignored him.

Nahbi of Naphtali gave a grim laugh. "That's *all* I plan to do."

"What good if we get ourselves killed?" Ammiel of Dan wanted to know.

Joshua looked across the fire at Caleb. Caleb gave him a hard stare. *Why do you say nothing? You, who have stood beside Moses. You, who have seen closer at hand than any of us the power of the Lord.*

The others talked on around them. "No one has to die if we keep out of the cities and stay off the roads."

"Stay low and listen," Caleb said in disgust. "Be like a lizard in the dust."

Shaphat's eyes flashed. "You are not our leader, Caleb. We will each do what is best in our own eyes."

Igal of Issachar, Gaddi of Manasseh, and Asher's Sethur agreed.

"You don't have to say much to plant fear in the minds of men, do you?" Caleb looked around the gathering, jaw clenched.

"We were not sent to be foolhardy. You're going to get yourself and anyone who travels with you killed!"

Caleb glared at Joshua. He looked up to the heavens. "These are the leaders of Israel?" He rose abruptly, unable to stomach any more, and went out into the night. He wanted to shout out his frustration at their timidity, but instead sat alone, thinking about God. He missed the swirling cloud of protection, the Word of God given through Moses. Even now that he had been chosen by God to stand among these men, Caleb felt like an outsider. Had he nothing in common with them? God's chosen! Cowards, every one.

He didn't understand Joshua's reticence. The young man had fought valiantly against the Amalekites. He was no coward. So why did he sit in silence, watching and listening, not an idea in his head?

Am I wrong, Lord? Should we creep along, peering over rocks and from behind trees? Should we tiptoe through the land? Should I go back to the fire and give in to their plans? I can't do that. I can't!

If I sit with them and take their counsel, I will give in to fear. I will cower before the Canaanites as I did the Egyptians. Who then will be master of my life but fear itself? Lord, You alone are to be feared. You are the One who holds our lives in Your hands.

Joshua joined him. "We leave at first light." He looked up, scanning the night sky. "They will go in three groups."

"Three groups and one alone."

"You and I will travel together."

"Did you decide that all by yourself, Joshua?" Caleb gave a cold laugh as he stood and faced him. "Or did the others decide for you? Did you all cast lots around the fire?"

"I needed to hear everyone's plan and then lay them out before the Lord to seek His guidance."

Temper snuffed by Joshua's words, Caleb rubbed the back of his neck. "Forgive me, brother." He gave a self-deprecating laugh. "No wonder God chose you to stand at Moses' side."

"I have much to learn, Caleb, but the Lord has said, 'Do not be afraid.'"

Caleb turned the younger man back toward the light. "Then we will not be afraid! We will cast out our fear of men, and fear only the Lord who holds our lives in His mighty hand."

+   +   +

The rugged mountains and wadis of the Negev made travel difficult. Two of the groups decided they would head for the foothills to the west, traveling in the forests below the ridge country. Caleb was relieved they were finally willing to venture out.

Caleb and Joshua moved farther north until they encountered towns of stone built on hilltops. They spent the night outside the walls of Kiriath-sepher, paid tariffs so they could trade, and set out wares at the marketplace the next day.

Caleb fought his fears as he watched the Hittite men. They stood a head taller than he and were heavier muscled. Armed and richly dressed from the cone helmets and thick braided hair and trimmed beards to their finely woven, colorfully patterned garments and leather-covered feet, they walked with an air of power and confidence. The women, too, were comely and bold.

"You do not speak as we do." A woman looked him over. "Where are you from?"

He noticed her interest in a gold and lapis bracelet, and picked it up. "Egypt. A ruined country." He held the bracelet out and named his price—grain, olive oil.

Others milled around the jewelry, bargaining. "Will apricots do? Or almonds?" Caleb agreed to a measure of both.

The first woman returned quickly with the necessary staples. Her eyes glowed as she slipped the bracelet on. "I got the better bargain." She laughed. "Grain we have in plenty, and olive oil, but nothing so grand as this." She caressed the gold and lapis. "What did you mean when you said Egypt is ruined?"

"The plagues."

"What plagues?" Another heard the dread word.

"The God of the Hebrews made war against the gods of Pharaoh. The Nile turned to blood. Frogs and flies swarmed over the country. Then locusts came and ate the crops. Fire from heaven burned what remained. Pestilence killed the cattle, sheep, goats, camels. Even as we began starving, an outbreak of boils struck everyone, even the house of Pharaoh, and then the worst came to pass. Have you ever had a boil?"

"No."

"Such pain and misery, you can't imagine. And the scars. Horrible."

"Scars?" The woman's eyes went wide with alarm. "You said that wasn't the worst. What could be worse than beauty destroyed?"

"Tell us." Another came close.

"What did you mean by the worst?"

"How could it be worse than what you have described?"

"The Lord God of Israel struck down every firstborn male from Pharaoh's house to the lowest servant, and even among the animals."

"Do you hear what this man says?" The woman called for others to listen. A crowd of men and women gathered.

"How did you survive?"

"We escaped death by the skin of our teeth." Caleb noted the weapon the man wore. "May I have a look at that sword?"

"Why? You have swords in Egypt."

"I have never seen anything so grand."

Proud, the man drew it, taunting Caleb for a moment before offering a closer look. Caleb took it carefully. "Such an honor." He flattered the owner as he studied the shape of the blade, tested the weight and balance, while the man laughed among his friends.

Caleb handed the sword to Joshua, who studied it as well and handed it back to the Hittite. "Perhaps it is a good time to expand our territories," the man said as he slipped the sword into its scabbard. "We will tell our king of Egypt's weakened state."

Caleb and Joshua took turns walking around the town, and then packed up their remaining wares and moved on.

"They have more gods than Egypt."

"Baser ones." Caleb couldn't hide his disgust. "Here I am, a stranger to their city, and one of their women invites me to please Astarte by lying with her."

"At least it was not Anath calling for your blood. These people bow down to gods who consume children in fires and call for men and women to fornicate upon their altars. Did you notice how little surprised those women were when you told them about the tenth plague and death of the firstborn? Some in Canaan cast their firstborn sons into the fire to appease Molech."

They traveled on to Kiriath-arba, a city inhabited by the sons of Anak, a descendant of giants. The land was good, the city walled and fortified. Altars stood on every corner, the largest in the middle of town. Caleb saw crowds gather to watch a man and woman writhe upon an altar, crying out for Baal to awaken and bring fertility to their land. Lust swept like fire among them. The more

Caleb saw of these people, the more he despised them for their debauchery and wickedness. There was no limit to the grotesque worship they performed for their gods—even to burning their own children.

He and Joshua traveled to a Jebusite city on the mountaintops, then on to Ai and Shechem until they reached Rehob in the far north. Turning south once again, they made their way down the mountains and traveled along a great rift and the River Jordan. Jericho loomed before them.

They followed the trade road into the mountains again, meeting the others at the prearranged point near Kiriath-arba. They all agreed that the land was everything God had promised, a land of milk with its flocks and herds, and of honey among the fruit trees and wheat fields and olive groves and vineyards. They had all tasted of it.

When they came through the valley, Caleb and Joshua cut a single cluster of grapes so large they had to carry it on a pole between them. "Go get some of those pomegranates," Joshua called to the others.

"And some figs!" Caleb shouted. He laughed. "The people will never believe the abundance until they see it with their own eyes. Even what we bring back will not tell them of the riches of the land God promised us."

Forty days had passed, and Caleb couldn't wait to get back to Kadesh. As soon as the people heard and saw proof that everything God had said was true, the sooner they would come back. God would help them drive out the evil inhabitants so the twelve tribes could reclaim the land Jacob's and Caleb's ancestors had left four hundred years ago.

Not once did it occur to Caleb that the people might not listen.

+ + +

"The spies are returning!" People hailed them. "They're here!" Men, women and children ran to them, gathering alongside, walking with them as they entered the camp. They exclaimed at the cluster of grapes. "Have you ever seen anything like that in your life?"

"This is just a small sample of what God is giving us," Caleb boasted in the Lord. "Forests, wheat fields, orchards, flocks of sheep and herds of cattle."

"And the people? What are the people like?"

"Tall," Palti said.

"Fierce. Warriors, all of them," Ammiel reported as he walked in.

Annoyed, Caleb called out loudly, "They are no threat for the Lord our God!"

Moses and Aaron and the seventy elders were waiting for them before the Tabernacle. Joshua and Caleb turned the pole so they approached straight on with the immense cluster of grapes suspended between them. Caleb grinned at their expressions and laughed with joy. Thousands came, pressing in, talking among themselves in excitement, peering at the men and the samples of the fruit of the land.

Moses raised his hands for silence. "Tell us what you learned."

Shaphat spoke quickly, joined by Igal, Palti, and Ammiel. "We arrived in the land you sent us to see, and it is indeed a magnificent country—a land flowing with milk and honey. Here is some of its fruit as proof. But the people living there are powerful, and their cities and towns are fortified and very large. We also saw the descendants of Anak who are living there!"

"Giants!" A ripple of alarm spread out among the gathering.

"The Amalekites live in the Negev."

"And the Hittites, Jebusites, and Amorites live in the hill country."

"The Canaanites live along the coast of the Mediterranean Sea and along the Jordan Valley."

The people grew restless, fear spreading through the crowd. "Giants . . . fortified cities . . . Anak . . ."

Caleb stepped forward and raised his hands. "Quiet. Listen, all of you." He did not shout. He knew he must hold his temper and speak as a father would to frightened children. "We were not sent to find out *if* we could take the land. The Lord has already given the land to us. All we have to do is obey Him. You remember what the Lord did to Egypt. Let's go at once to take the land. We can certainly conquer it!"

The other spies spoke loudly, breaking in on his appeal. "We can't go up against them!"

"They are stronger than we are!"

"Listen to us!"

"What do we know about war?"

"We are only slaves!"

"They are seasoned warriors!"

Caleb shouted over them. "We can take the land! Don't be afraid of those people."

"Don't listen to this man. He's not even a Hebrew!"

Men cried out. "He stands for Judah! Caleb stands for Judah!"

Emboldened, Caleb shouted louder. "It is a beautiful land. Green fields and hills, cities already built and ready for us to take!"

"The land we explored will swallow up any who go
to live there!"

"All the people we saw were huge!"

"We even saw giants there, the descendants of Anak!"

"We felt like grasshoppers next to them, and that's
what we looked like to them!"

"The land is ours!" Caleb cried out. "The Lord has
already given it to us!"

Moses called for order. He looked old and tired as he
told the people to return to their tents and allow the elders
to talk among themselves. He and Aaron turned away,
dejected, and the elders followed. The people cried out
their disappointment and wandered away, weeping.

Furious, Caleb grabbed Joshua by the arm. "Why
didn't you speak up? Why did you stand silent?"

"There are two million people and ten shouting to be
heard. They wouldn't have heard me."

"You know as well as I do the land is ours. God said He
would give it to us. Where is your faith, Joshua? Where is
the courage I saw in the battle against the Amalekites?
Where is that assurance I saw in Canaan? Those others are
cowards. We cannot let them sway the people. You hold a
high position. People will listen to you! Are you going to
speak out or not? Decide, Joshua! Will you lead the congregation or follow?"

"I'm not the leader, Caleb. Moses is."

"For now, yes. And as his assistant, you can speak to
him. But will you have the guts to do so? Why do you
think God placed you beside Moses? Think, man. When
Moses goes to his fathers, who will stand in his place? His
half-Midianite sons? Korah, who would like to take us
back to Egypt? God is preparing *you* to lead. How is it I

can see it and you can't? For God and the sake of the people, *stand and be heard!*" Caleb let go of the younger man and strode through the camp to his tent.

When he ducked and entered his tent, he found his entire family sitting in a circle. He could feel their tension, see their doubt. Only Ephrathah's eyes shone with something other than fear. "Tell them what you saw, my husband. Tell them about the Promised Land."

And so he did, relieved as he saw their fears turn to hope and then excitement. He reminded them of what God had done to Egypt in order to deliver them from slavery. "He is a mighty God. Nothing is too difficult for Him. But we must trust Him. We must be ready so that when He tells us to go into Canaan, *we go!*"

With Ephrathah's encouragement, they kept him talking about the beauty of Canaan most of the night.

But outside his tent, beyond his cloistered family members, out there among the thousands upon thousands, the seed of fear had taken root and was spreading its malevolent tendrils through the camp, stifling anticipation, smothering joy, and bringing a wave of murderous wrath.

✦   ✦   ✦

When Caleb finally stretched out to rest, he slept fitfully. People wailed in the distance. He awakened once to shouts in the darkness. What had the people expected? That the Lord would wipe out everyone *before* they reached the borders of Canaan, so they could enter unoccupied land? He got up before sunrise, washed, and dressed in his best clothing.

Ephrathah heard him moving about the tent and rose.

She awakened the others. "Hurry. We must go with your father. Come, Jerioth. We must stand behind our husband."

Caleb pushed aside the curtain. "Stay here." Both women were pregnant, and he didn't want any harm to come to them or the babies they carried. "The people are angry. I don't know what will happen. It's best if you both remain here rather than be caught up in their rebellion."

"What would you have us do?"

"Pray to the Lord our God that the people will listen and obey the Lord."

Thousands were coming from every area of the camp, marching and shouting. Caleb ran ahead and pressed his way through those who had already gathered before the Tabernacle. He shoved his way through the crowd and broke free at the front, running to stand beside Joshua. "We have to stop them from rebelling!"

"What have you done to us, Moses?"

"We wish we had died in Egypt!"

"Or even here in the wilderness!"

"Why is the Lord taking us to this country only to have us die in battle?"

"Our wives and little ones will be carried off as slaves!"

"We should go back!"

Elders from the tribes came to the front, the ten other scouts among them. Red-faced men shouted, "Let's choose a leader and go back to Egypt!"

Crying out in fear, Moses and Aaron dropped to the ground before the people. Caleb understood, for he felt the change in the air around him. It was not just fear of the people that made them prostrate themselves. Were the people so foolish they didn't know the Lord heard them crying to go back to the land from which He had delivered them? to go back to slavery? to go back to false gods and idols?

Caleb let out a cry and ripped his garment. While Moses and Aaron covered their heads in fear of what the Lord would do, Caleb dove into the fracas, shouting with all his strength, "Listen, you people! Listen! The land we explored is wonderful land!"

Joshua shouted with him. "If the Lord is pleased with us, He will bring us safely into that land and give it to us!"

Caleb strode toward the elders and scouts, pointing at them. "Do not rebel against the Lord, and don't be afraid of the people of the land."

"They are only helpless prey to us!" Joshua shouted. "They have no protection, but the Lord is with us!"

"*The Lord is with us!*"

"Don't be afraid of them!"

Korah stepped forward. "Don't listen to this *Caleb!* He and Moses' lackey would lead you into a land filled with enemies who have the power to slay your little ones."

"Do you want to be slaughtered?"

"No!"

"*Stone them!*"

Caleb saw the hatred in the people's faces, the fury growing past reason as they scraped around on the ground for rocks and pebbles.

Is this where my faith has led me, Lord? To death? Then let it be.

Screams rent the air and people scattered, for the cloud moved, changing color as it rose, spread, compressed, descended, and stood between the people and Caleb and Joshua. Caleb threw himself to the ground, covering his head in terror. Joshua lay beside him, crying out to God not to kill everyone.

Moses cried out, too. "*Oh, Lord, no!*" Moses was on his feet, hands raised, pleading frantically. "What will the Egyptians think when they hear about it?"

About what? Caleb's heart pounded. He felt the presence of the Lord, the rising wrath, the chill of death close at hand. He shook violently and clutched the earth.

"The Egyptians know full well the power You displayed in rescuing these people from Egypt!" Moses cried out to the Lord. "They will tell this to the inhabitants of this land, who are well aware that You are with this people. They know, Lord, that You have appeared in full view of Your people in the pillar of cloud that hovers over them. They know that You go before them in the pillar of cloud by day and the pillar of fire by night."

Never had Caleb heard Moses speak so fast. He felt judgment at hand. *Oh, Lord, have mercy upon us. Speak faster, Moses. Plead for us. God hears your voice. Without you, the Lord will kill us. My children! My wives!*

"Now if You slaughter all these people . . ."

People screamed and scattered.

" . . . if You slaughter all these people, the nations that have heard of Your fame will say, 'The Lord was not able to bring them into the land He swore to give them, so He killed them in the wilderness.'"

Wailing rose. Thousands of voices cried out in terror, "Save us, Moses!"

Caleb wanted to rise up and scream to the people, "Cry to the Lord, for it is He who saves!" Were they still so foolish they could not hear Moses' pleading? "Cry out to the Lord for forgiveness."

"*Please*, Lord, prove that Your power is as great as You have claimed it to be." Moses held his hands high. "For You said, 'The Lord is slow to anger and rich in unfailing love, forgiving every kind of sin and rebellion. Even so He does not leave sin unpunished, but He punishes the children for the sins of their parents to the third and fourth generations.' Please pardon the sins of this people because of Your magnificent, unfailing love, just as You have forgiven them ever since they left Egypt."

Moses went down on his face before the Lord, and there was silence, such a silence that Caleb's ears rang with it. And then he thought he heard a still, quiet Voice whisper his name like a breath of warm, life-giving air. He strained mentally toward that Voice, listening intently, yearning to hear it again, so soft and loving but with the power of Almighty God behind it. But it was not for him to hear more. Not yet. Not now.

Stretching out his arms on the ground, his face in the dust, Caleb prayed. *Lord, Lord, if You slay me now because I failed to convince these people of what I saw, I will die happy because it is by Your hand my life ends.*

The glorious presence of the Lord lifted. Moses sobbed in relief.

Caleb raised his head as the old man rose slowly to his feet, trembling, tears running into his white beard. But when Moses looked out at the people, his eyes blazed. Caleb felt fear then, a fear that welled up inside him and made his stomach quiver, sweat bead, his mouth go dry.

"Listen, all of you, and hear the Word of the Lord!" The power of the Lord was behind Moses' voice and it carried like a storm.

Caleb moved quickly so that he was standing beside

Joshua again. The other ten scouts did not join them, but remained among the elders of their tribes. There might as well have been a chasm between them. On one side stood six hundred thousand men who had chosen to fear the enemy rather than follow their trusted Friend. They had chosen to speak against the One who had saved them and provided for them every day since they had been rescued from slavery. On the other side stood Caleb and Joshua, two strong voices of reason not heeded.

The people came closer, but rebellion still shone in their eyes. The elders of each tribe came to the front with their scout. Caleb looked out at them and wondered how they could think the threat was past, that the Lord would do whatever Moses asked.

We deserve nothing, Lord. After all You have done for us, and this is what the people decide.

"Hear the Word of the Lord!" Moses' voice went forth like fire. "'I will pardon them as you have requested. But as surely as I live, and as surely as the earth is filled with the Lord's glory, not one of these people will ever enter that land.'"

The Promised Land was lost to them. While many cried out in relief, Caleb cried out in grief and fell upon his face again. He drew his knees up under his body and threw dust on his head. Imagining the ten scouts, he pounded the earth with his fists and wept bitterly.

Moses voice rose, hot with anger, weighed with grief.

"'They have seen My glorious presence and the miraculous signs I performed both in Egypt and in the wilderness, but again and again they tested Me by refusing to listen. They will never even see the land I swore to give their ancestors. None of those who have treated Me with contempt will enter it.'"

Moses paused and then spoke tenderly. "'But my servant Caleb . . .'"

My servant Caleb . . . The Voice again, so tenderly calling him. **Caleb, My servant** . . .

Caleb raised his face to the heavens. Moses spoke, but it was the Lord's voice Caleb heard. **Caleb is different from the others. He has remained loyal to Me, and I will bring him into the land he explored. His descendants will receive their full share of that land.**

Caleb bowed his face to the ground. *Unworthy, Lord, I am an unworthy dog.*

What of Joshua?

"'Now, *turn around,*'" Moses said in the power of the Spirit, "'and don't go on toward the land where the Amalekites and Canaanites live. Tomorrow you must set out for the wilderness in the direction of the Red Sea.'"

The people wailed, but some stood their ground.

"No. We want our land."

Caleb covered his head. It was never *their* land. It had always been the Lord's land. And it was the Lord who would have placed them there as He had placed Adam and Eve in the Garden of Eden. *Why do men always refuse to listen and act upon what the Lord says? Lord, give me the heart to hear and the courage to obey.*

"Thus says the Lord, 'How long will this wicked nation complain about Me? I have heard everything the Israelites have been saying. You will all die here in this wilderness! Because you complained against Me, none of you who are twenty years old or older and were counted in the census

will enter the land I swore to give you. The only exceptions will be Caleb and Joshua.

"'You said your children would be taken captive. Well,
I will bring *them* safely into the land, and they will enjoy
what you have despised. But as for you, your dead bodies
will fall in this wilderness. And your children will be like
shepherds, wandering in the wilderness forty years. In
this way, they will pay for your faithlessness, until the last
of you lies dead in the wilderness.'"

The people drew back from Moses as he came forward,
hands spread, his voice carrying over the throng. "'Because
the men who explored the land were there for forty days,
you must wander in the wilderness for forty years—a year
for each day, suffering the consequences of your sins. You
will discover what it is like to have Me for an enemy.'"

Gagging violently, Palti fell to the ground in convul-
sions. People screamed and withdrew as Palti bit off his
own tongue. People ran from Shaphat, who dropped
where he stood among the elders. Igal and Gaddiel pitched
over. Ammiel ran, Gaddi on his heels, but both fell as
though struck by invisible arrows. Sethur and Nahbi,
Geuel and Shammua died as Palti did.

Of the twelve who had explored the land, only Caleb
and Joshua stood untouched by God's judgment, for they
hadn't spread lies about the land and its people.

Caleb shook as the Lord took swift vengeance. The people scattered, but still God's hand of judgment was upon
them, and many others died that night.

In the morning, hundreds went out with their weapons
to take Canaan. "Let's go," they said. "We realize that we
have sinned, but now we are ready to enter the land the
Lord has promised us."

"What are you doing?" Moses ran after them, Joshua with him. "God has told us to turn back to the Red Sea!"

"We're not going back to the Sinai. The Lord said He would give us the land, and we're going to take it."

But Moses said, "Why are you now disobeying the Lord's orders to return to the wilderness? It won't work. Do not go into the land now. You will only be crushed by your enemies because the Lord is not with you. When you face the Amalekites and Canaanites in battle, you will be slaughtered. The Lord will abandon you because you have abandoned the Lord!"

"Who are you to tell us to stay here? We're sick of you telling us what not to do and what to do. We *will* take the land. God *will* help us."

Caleb stood at the edge of camp, watching several of his friends head north for Canaan. They had fretted and argued all night, and finally convinced themselves they could do it. They thought there was power in their dream, power to reach out and grab what they wanted for themselves.

He had heard his brother say, "If we just believe we can do it, it will happen."

They assumed God would give in to *their* desire and bless *their* endeavors. Faith in God would have given them everything they ever hoped to have, but faith in themselves would bring them death.

Caleb shouted after them, "When will you learn to obey the Lord?"

One of his brothers shouted back, "Come with us, Caleb. When will you learn it is not the Lord who speaks, but Moses! And who is he to tell us what to do?"

Helpless, angry, Caleb stood his ground. "Fools! All of

you!" His eyes hot, Caleb dropped to his knees and hung his head. Someone gripped his shoulder.

Joshua watched the rebels. "When they are dead, the others will heed the Word of the Lord."

Caleb gave a laugh of despair. "Do you really think so? Like begets like. Their children will be just like them."

"Your voice is filled with hatred."

"I hate those who hate Moses. To hate God's prophet is to hate God Himself. I hate them with a passion almost as great as my love for God!"

"Brother . . ."

"It sears my heart," Caleb cried out in wrath. "We were so close. So close! And their faithlessness has stripped us bare. Now, you and I must wait forty years to enter into the land God gave us. Forty years, Joshua! My sons and little ones will suffer in the desert because of them. Our wives will die without ever seeing what you and I saw." He grasped Joshua's garment. "And I see it in your eyes, too, my friend."

"It chews at my soul. What must we do about it?"

Caleb gripped the robe over Joshua's heart. "Go back." He shut his eyes and spoke quietly, in despair. "Go back to the last place where we rejoiced over God our Savior. Go back to the Red Sea and begin again."

And God preserve us, may we continue in faith this time.

THREE

THE congregation hadn't even traveled toward the Red Sea for a day when another rebellion broke out, this time led by Korah, a Levite who blamed Moses for the deaths of those who had gone into the Promised Land. He scorned Aaron as high priest and roused others to think likewise. Two hundred and fifty Levites stood with Korah, determined to preside over worship. Moses told them to stand at the entrances of their tents with censors of burning incense the next morning and the Lord would decide.

Struck by fire from the Holy of Holies, Korah and his rebels died horribly. The earth opened with a roar and swallowed them, along with their households. Tumbling down into the yawning jaws of Sheol, they screamed, as the jagged edges of the precipice closed over them like the teeth of a lion.

And still, it was not enough to put an end to the stubbornness of hearts baked and hardened to stone beneath the sun of Egypt's profane and profligate gods.

"Stay away from the people." Caleb kept his wives and children inside the tent. "Stay out of it." He could feel the heat of rebellion building all around him, even in the tribe of Judah as people wailed and cried out through the night.

"I can't bear it!" Ephrathah covered her ears.

The people rose up again, and accused Moses of killing God's people. The glory of the Lord appeared and struck the camp with plague. Men and women blaspheming God and His prophet dropped dead where they stood. Ten, a hundred, a thousand, thousands upon thousands. The rebels could not run and hide, for God knew them and

sought them out for destruction. Moses cried out for
mercy and sent Aaron running to burn incense to atone
for the people. Aaron ran to do what was asked of him,
and stood between the living and the dead.

Finally, the people were silent, too afraid to open their
mouths lest another plague fall upon them. Too late, they
remembered what the Lord had done in Egypt. If not for
Moses and Aaron, they would all be dead.

Caleb came out of hiding to help carry Judah's dead
from the camp. But he knew it wasn't over. "I can see it
in their eyes."

Ephrathah put her arm around him in the darkness of
their tent. "What do you see, my love?" She pressed into
the shelter of his arm.

"Wrath. But it isn't for those who rebelled against the
Lord, but against God Himself for holding true to His
word." It was as though the muddy waters of the Nile still
ran in their veins, his included, for Caleb knew sin dwelt
in him. He loved these men who had become his brothers.
He loved them, and yet, he hated them, too. When he
heard a man grumbling close by, he could have so easily
raised his hand against him and struck him down. Resentment rose, bringing with it a lust for vengeance.

*My heart is a storm within me, Lord. You are my God!
Let nothing stand between You and me. Sin crouches at the
entrance of my heart waiting to devour me. And I must fight
against it. Oh, God, how I must fight against the fire in my
blood! Their faithlessness kept me and my sons from Canaan.
Help me not to hate these people. Help me to stand firm
beneath the cooling spring of Your living water so that I may
obey Your every command whether I understand or not.*

But the grumbling persisted, low, an undercurrent that

still pulled at the souls of some, sucking the hope from God's promises.

Bowing his head, Caleb gripped the hoe he used to dig graves until his fingers hurt.

Help me, Lord. Oh, God, help me not to give in to my wrath.

✦ ✦ ✦

The multitude followed the Lord and Moses back to the Red Sea, and then the wandering began. No one knew how long they would remain in one place. Caleb kept his eyes on the cloud, for when it rose, so too did he and his family members. "Rise up. The Lord is on the move. *Rise up!*"

Jerioth bore another son. Caleb named him for the place where God allowed them to camp. When Ephrathah bore a son, Caleb lifted him high before the cloud of the Lord. "His name will be Hur."

Hezron stood bent over his staff. "Another name not of our family." The years were heavy upon him, and the grief of sons lost spawned bitterness and hatred.

Caleb did not weaken. "Hur and Aaron held Moses' arms up while Joshua went out against Amalek. So shall my son support those who are chosen of God to lead the people." He held the babe against his heart. "My sons shall choose honor over shame."

"May they grow strong in faith like you, but have Moses' compassion." The old man walked away.

Caleb kept his sons close, even in the midst of Judah, not wanting them to mingle among those who still looked back toward Egypt and sighed.

Zimri sought him out. "We need you in the council of elders."

"To what purpose?" They had never listened to him before.

"Your enemies have died, my friend, many in the plague."

Caleb lifted his head. "And should I mourn them?"

"You heard their screams just as I did. I lost sons that day. Have you no pity for me or those the Lord killed?"

"It was their own faithlessness that brought them down."

"Dreams too long delayed in coming."

Even Zimri was blind. "It was not a dream! The land was there as God promised, ripe as the grapes and pome-granates Joshua and I brought back to you. And your fear hardened your heart against the Lord."

"My sons, my sons. Only Carmi and his son are left."

Caleb saw the appeal in the old man's eyes, but would not give in to it. "Faithless still, Zimri. You make excuses for blasphemers. You have heard the Law. Love the Lord your God with all your heart and all your soul and with all your might. You and the others still hold fast to flesh and blood."

"You resent us so much?"

"I resent the years of waste."

Zimri looked at the young men playing games. His mouth drew tight. "You will go in to that which we have been denied."

"Yes. When I'm *eighty*. When my infant sons are as old as I am now. Mesha and Mareshah will be older still!"

Zimri hung his head.

Caleb turned away, but Zimri grasped his arm. "We *need* you." He looked up, his eyes moist. "My grandsons need you."

So Caleb went to the council of elders. "You want to hear what I have to say? So be it. Stop talking among yourselves and *listen* to the Lord God who brought you out of Egypt. It is too late to look back on what could have been. We must look forward to the promise God has given us. Yes. You will all die! But your sons will go into Canaan—if they learn to obey the Lord. When you come together, judge cases wisely according to the Law. When you gather, speak of the miracles you saw in Egypt. Speak of the opening of the Red Sea; speak of the water that came forth from the rock. Give thanks over the manna you receive from God's hand each morning. Give thanks for the pillar of fire that protects us by night. Confess to your sons and daughters that it is by our own sins that we wander in this desert. It is because we did not trust in the Lord that they must live as nomads! Let them see us humble ourselves before the Lord so that they will learn *He is the Lord our God!* We failed to obey. We must teach our sons to succeed."

Silent, the men looked to Zimri and he spoke for them all. "We agree, Caleb. Only promise you will lead them."

Caleb looked around the circle. Still, after everything, they failed to understand. "No. I will not. For the Lord our God will lead them!"

✦ ✦ ✦

The men sent their sons to Caleb, who pressed them hard. He walked down their ranks.

"We no longer have fields to plow and plant, nor crops to harvest, for the Lord has given us all we need. You do not have to toil in the sun making bricks as your fathers did before you. But you will not spend your days in idleness! The Lord is a warrior, the Lord is His Name!"

"The Lord is a warrior, the Lord is His Name!" his sons called out. The others joined in.

"Again. And mean it!"

They shouted.

"We will all learn to be warriors as well." He set courses for them to run to make their bodies strong and fast. He planned games to test their agility and strength. He drilled them and drilled them. The older men watched and died as their sons trained.

Caleb's sons and the others with them were sprouting up like ripe stalks of wheat. But Caleb wanted them strong and unwavering. "You will not bend with every wind that blows down upon us. There were cedars in Canaan, towers of strength. So shall we be. We will stand firm in the power of the Lord our God!"

Whenever the Lord settled the people in a place with wood, Caleb sent out his sons to gather it and build up the fires. The clang of metal against metal and hiss of steam was heard around his camp as he beat his plowshares into swords and his pruning hooks into spears. Through trial and error, the young men learned to wield the weapons and hit the mark with bow and arrow. The shepherds among them taught others how to use the sling and stones.

"Keep your eyes on the Lord," Caleb taught them. "Be ready to set out the moment the cloud lifts from the Tabernacle." He taught the boys and young men to run at the first blast of the shofar, rewarding those who were first to have their camps ready for the journey to the next site.

"Rise up! *Rise up, O Israel!* The Lord is on the move!" And so they all learned to do, not reluctantly but swiftly, pulling down tents, rolling, packing, setting out to wherever God led them.

One of Caleb's sons was always on watch. For he wanted Judah close on Moses' and Aaron's heels, within sight of Joshua who would one day lead.

+ + +

Caleb and Joshua often worshiped together and then went to a high place that gave them an overview of the camp. Thousands of tents spread out over the desert plain beneath a canopy of cloud. Smoke rose from cook fires. Children ran between the tents; old men gathered at entrances while women served. Where Judah camped, young men sparred and raced against one another. In the distance, shepherds moved flocks of sheep and herds of cattle closer for the night.

The air began to change. Caleb held his breath and watched the transformation of cooling cloud to swirling pillar of flame. It never ceased to amaze him. "Shadowed by day, warmed by night. Our Lord is ever merciful."

Joshua made a sound of agreement. "You are training Judah's sons to become fierce warriors."

Caleb could detect neither approval nor reprimand in Joshua's statement. "All the sons of Jacob should train to be warriors."

"I've been praying on the matter."

"And what does the Lord say?"

"He speaks to Moses, not to me." Caleb felt Joshua's restlessness and knew he had more to say. After a long moment, Joshua glanced at him. "Nothing has been said one way or the other, which gives me great cause to wonder."

"About what?"

"Whether it is right to train for battle."

"When the Lord sends us into Canaan, Joshua, we must

know how to fight. Do you think it a sin to train soldiers?"

"The Lord said the land is ours."

"Yes. The victory is already decided, but our work has yet to be done. Do you think the Lord would have us recline on mats and sleep for the next forty years?"

"Our work is to believe, Caleb."

"Yes, Joshua, but faith is proven by action. The ten scouts who went with us into Canaan believed in God, but they refused to act upon their faith by leading their brothers into Canaan." He sneered. "Perhaps they would have had the courage had God crushed the walls of the fortified cities and obliterated the people *before* extending the invitation to us to occupy the land."

"You have no compassion for them."

Caleb clenched his teeth.

"They suffered for their lack of faith, Caleb."

"Their lack of faith could grow within our ranks. Inactivity breeds rebellion. We must do something. What better than to prepare for the battle ahead?"

"You speak as though we are soldiers or charioteers. We are slaves."

"We *were* slaves. Now we are free men with God's promise of a future and a hope. The children born to us in the wilderness will never have known the yoke of Egypt. They will be born beneath the canopy of God. They will walk in His presence every day of their lives. Perhaps it is for us who spent most of our lives bowing down to others to learn to be like our children. If I am bound to anyone as slave, it is to the Lord our God. You must not weaken, Joshua. You must not allow yourself to look back, but up." He pointed to the pillar of fire. "And out to what is before us." He pointed north to Canaan.

"It is the wandering that wears upon me."

"As it wears upon us all. But it is a training ground, too." Caleb looked toward the horizon. Would God rise up tomorrow and lead them somewhere else? Only the Lord could lead them through this wasteland and bring them to water. "We may believe we wander aimlessly, my friend, but I am convinced God has a plan. I must believe or I would despair. We were judged and now we live with the consequences of our sins, but surely this isn't all about punishment. Every day we keep our eyes upon Him, we are learning to move when He moves."

"It is punishment."

"Yes. Yes." Caleb grew impatient. "But it is also opportunity." He had thought much about it over the past weeks. "Perhaps God always has more than one purpose. He judged us righteously, but He shows us mercy. He gives us the Law on which to fix our minds and hearts, a Law that sets me at war within myself. And God told us to sacrifice every morning and evening. The smell is a constant reminder. He knows us so well. He gives us food and water to sustain us. He directs our every step. When the Lord rises up, we strike our tents and follow. When He returns to the Tabernacle, we camp and wait. In Egypt, our taskmasters did our thinking for us and we responded like beasts of burden. Now, we must think as men. We are not animals that graze at whatever pasture is available to us. We are faced with choices. Do we grumble among ourselves, or walk the path God has given us?"

Caleb pointed northeast. "That land is ours. Right now, it is filled with people who bow down to false gods and

practice all manner of evil. Every man, woman, and child
is corrupt and rotten with sin. You saw how they worshiped their gods, casting babies into fire and fornicating
on altars in the middle of town and under every spreading
oak. They practice worse abominations than Egypt all
puffed up and spread out like a cobra. The Lord sent
us into the land as scouts to see what we would be up
against. We saw. We know. Now, we must prepare to
do battle."

Joshua said nothing. Silence had never sat well upon
Caleb. He had no reason to doubt Joshua's courage, but he
wished he knew what was going on in his mind. "We have
fought battles before, Joshua. The Lord didn't tell us to sit
by and watch while He destroyed the Amalekites. He sent
us into battle against them."

"Moses prayed."

"And God answered by giving us victory."

"Sometimes we are called to do nothing more than pray,
Caleb."

"Yes. But is it wise to assume the Lord will destroy
Canaan with plagues first and then send us into the land?
Or wiser to train and prepare for whatever God asks of
us?" Even if the Lord told them to stand and watch, the
work would not be wasted if they were prepared to do
whatever God asked of them.

"You have already made up your mind about what we
should do."

Caleb looked down at the camps spread upon the plain.
Where the tents of Judah were positioned, youths fought
mock battles. After each rally, they backed off and began
again. "Are you trying to change it?"

"Where is prayer in all this strife?"

"Strife?" Caleb's jaw tightened. "There is less strife among the Judean boys who train than I've witnessed among the other tribes who do little more than gather manna every morning, then sit on their haunches and talk the rest of the day. Aimless talk leads to whining and complaining and rebellion. And as to prayer, it comes first. No one lifts a hand or a weapon until after morning sacrifices and the reading of the Law."

Joshua's mouth curved wryly. "But you are partial."

His temper bubbled. "Partial?"

"You show particular attention to certain men."

Why was Joshua pressing him so? Why didn't he just speak what was on his mind? "What are you getting at, Joshua?"

"You train the sons of Judah."

"Of course."

"You have other allegiances."

Caleb felt the heat surge into his face. Did he mean Edom? Caleb stared hard at Joshua through narrowed eyes. "My only allegiance is to the Lord who told me I will go into the land. When that day comes, I want my sons beside me, ready to destroy *anyone* or *anything* that stands in the way of our inheritance."

Joshua put his hand on Caleb's shoulder. "But you are *Hebrew,* my friend. A son of Abraham, and all these others are our brothers."

"Why bait me? Speak your mind."

"What has been in your mind has been on mine as well. We must train for battle. What troubles me is the way we're going about it. Scattered groups, scattered efforts. One day we may be at one another's throats rather than set against the enemies of God."

The vision caught Caleb's heart. He gripped Joshua's arm. "Then unite us!"

"It is not my place to do that."

"Then speak to Moses. The Lord brought twelve tribes together and brought them out of Egypt. Surely He wants us to be one flock and not twelve. Moses can also train us. He grew up in the Egyptian court among the princes. Much of his education must have centered on tactics and weaponry. And you are closer to him than his own sons, close enough to pose the question."

"You would have me be presumptuous?"

"If you do not ask, you will not receive an answer."

"And what if he says no?"

Caleb did not want to speak rashly. He looked out over the thousands of tents. He could see the banners of each tribe, the space between, boundaries. "Look at us. You are correct. We are scattered in our thinking. God is trying to bring us together through the Law—one mind, one heart, one promise that gives us hope. We cannot be twelve tribes encamped around the Tabernacle. We must become one nation under God! And every nation has an army. Let us build an army for the Lord." He looked into Joshua's solemn face. Joshua had aged greatly during the last months. Love for the people weighed heavily upon the younger man's heart.

"Speak to Moses, Joshua. Tell him what is on your mind and heart. I'm surprised you haven't already done so."

"He is troubled in spirit and prays unceasingly for the people."

"Who are vain and bored and need something to occupy them. *Ask!* You know what Moses will do."

"He will go to the Lord."

Caleb laughed joyously. "Yes!" He slapped Joshua hard on the back. "And then we will know if the fire in our blood was placed there by our own pride or by God's Spirit."

+   +   +

The years passed slowly as the Israelites moved from place to place in the wilderness. The slave generation died one by one as the children grew taller and more robust. Families were left without patriarchs and matriarchs, then without aunts and uncles.

Caleb faced constant sorrow as he watched friends and family members die. Zimri was the first, followed soon after by Hezron. Some died embittered and unrepentant. Others grieved over their lack of faith and its cost to their children. Zimri's son Carmi sat on the council now with Caleb. They became good, if not close, friends.

When Caleb walked among the tents, those of his generation watched him pass. Some stared with resentment, others with burning envy, precious few with a respectful nod of greeting. The camp was in constant mourning, over loved ones dying as well as over the sin that kept them from the Promised Land.

Boys clamored around Caleb wherever he went, eager to join in the training. He tested their knowledge of the Law first. "It is not enough to want to fight. All men have it in them to fight! You must know the One who leads you into battle."

"Moses!"

"And Joshua!"

Caleb knew what both men would say to that. "Go back

to your tent. You're not ready." They came to him with the
fire to fight, but without faith and knowledge. The Lord
was their commander. They must prepare their hearts and
minds to follow His will. Not a man's. Not even his.

The seventy elders died and were replaced by younger
men who lived with the cost of their fathers' sins. They
listened to Moses' counsel and acted upon it, choosing
wise men who loved the Lord to judge the people. One by
one, the men who grew up in the fear of Pharaoh died off
and were replaced by men who grew up in the fear of the
Lord.

The camps moved with the precision of an army. When
the cloud rose, so too did the people, often even before
the shofar blasted. The people were learning day by day,
week by week, month by month, year by year to keep
watch and follow the Lord.

The old moaned and mourned, grumbled and groaned,
and died.

The young praised and practiced, rejoiced in and rever-
enced God, and lived.

+   +   +

During the thirty-eighth year of wandering, Caleb was
called to the tent of Kenaz. His brother lay dying. Caleb sat
beside him, grieving this loss more than any other.

Kenaz smiled weakly. "I thought, perhaps, the Lord had
forgotten about me, and I might sneak into the Promised
Land among my sons and grandsons. . . ."

Caleb couldn't speak. He gripped Kenaz's hand between
his own.

"I have watched you, my brother." Kenaz's voice was
barely a whisper. "You sit at the entrance of your tent and

fix your eyes upon the pillar of fire. And God's fire is reflected in your eyes, my brother."

Caleb bowed his head, tears flowing.

"We should've listened . . ." Kenaz sighed. His hand went slack between Caleb's.

Two days later, Jerioth died, and a month later Caleb awakened to find Ephrathah dead beside him. A cry rose from his throat as he tore his clothing and went out to throw dust in the air. He didn't speak a word to anyone for a month.

Never had Caleb felt such a weight of grief upon him, and rebellion rose up with it, unbidden and unexpected. He ran to the Tabernacle and prostrated himself before the Lord. *Kill the evil within me, Lord. Kill it before it takes root and grows.* He did not leave the Tabernacle for three days. Still grieving, he rose with a peace beyond understanding. *The Lord, the Lord is my strength. He is my high place, my comfort.*

The next morning, the cloud moved and Caleb had his tents struck, packed, and set out to follow. When the Lord stopped, the Tabernacle was set up and the tribes took positions around it, this time at an oasis with date palms. As Caleb returned to the courtyard of the Tabernacle, he rested in the Lord's presence rather than warring within himself. Better was one day in the court of the Lord than a thousand elsewhere.

He mourned for Ephrathah, but went back out to train the young men for battle. A new generation had come to manhood, with sons coming up behind them. Caleb felt renewed strength flood through his body, as though the Lord had given him back the time and strength the wilderness had taken from him.

The forty years were almost over. Their wandering was almost at an end.

✦   ✦   ✦

The Lord led the Israelites to Kadesh a second time. Caleb gathered his sons and their sons around him. "This is where the people waited while Joshua and I went into Canaan. This is where the people rebelled against the Lord." He made fists. "Listen this time. Listen and obey."

He awakened each morning, prepared to go on, to move closer, to have that which God had promised him. Land of his own, a place to plant crops, a place where he could rest beneath his own olive tree and sip the fruit of his vines.

But the waiting wasn't over.

Moses' sister, Miriam, died. Shocked, the entire camp mourned her death as they would a mother. Something broke within the ranks and a mob cried out against Moses, for once again there was no water.

"The Lord will provide!" Caleb shouted, but no one listened. He went into his tent, and sat, head in hands.

If I stay out there, Lord, I will kill someone. I will draw my sword and not stop until You strike me down! Will we never change? Are we destined to rebel against the Lord God Almighty all our lives. Israel! The name itself means to wrestle with You. Is that why You called them that? This generation is the same as the last. Rebellion against God is in the blood!

Cries of jubilation came. He arose and went out to find water pouring from a rock. The people shouted and sang and splashed the water over themselves. The waters were called Meribah because this place was yet another where the Israelites had quarreled with the Lord. But after that day, Moses looked old and sick, and spoke hardly at all.

Moses sent messengers to Edom requesting passage through their land, and Edom answered with the threat of war. Caleb was filled with shame. Were the Edomites not brothers? They—like Caleb—were descended from Esau. Caleb despised the blood that ran in his veins.

Once again, Moses sent messengers with assurances that the people would stay to the King's Highway and not tread upon any field or go through any vineyard or even drink water from any well, but merely pass through to the land God had given them. Not only did the Edomites refuse, they came out with an army ready for battle.

"Tell Moses we are ready to fight!" Caleb told Joshua. "Send us out to deal with these people. Let none stand in the way of the Lord God of Israel!"

"They are brothers, Caleb."

"They reject us. Let us annihilate them! They are betrayers and blasphemers."

"They are descendants of Abraham as we are."

"They are a wall between us and God's promises!"

"Caleb—"

"Do not excuse them, Joshua. Men must choose. And they have chosen death!"

"You are my brother and friend, Caleb. Remember the Law. Vengeance is the Lord's."

The words pierced Caleb and cooled his anger. But his temper and impatience rose again when Moses prayed and then turned away from Edom and set out to return to Kadesh.

"Kadesh!" Caleb ground his teeth. "Will our faith take us no farther than Kadesh?" When the people rested, he went to the Tabernacle and spent the night on his face in the dust. *Why, Lord? Why must we show mercy?*

They moved on to Mount Hor and made camp. Moses, Aaron, and Aaron's son Eleazar went up the mountain. Caleb's impatience was eating him alive. He practiced with his sword. He paced. He pondered. *Lord, Lord! When? The slaves are all dead! Your judgment has been fulfilled!*

Only Moses and Eleazar came down.

When word spread that Aaron was dead, shock spread through the camp and the people went into mourning. No one had expected God to take Aaron. Thirty days passed before the cloud rose and the people followed Him along the road to Atharim.

Shouts and screams came from the distance. Armed and ready to fight, Caleb shouted for his sons. But it was already too late. Canaanites living in the Negev, led by the king of Arad, had attacked and taken captives. The people mourned and raged. It had happened so quickly, no one had expected it.

Caleb's wrath boiled over. "Give us leave to destroy them."

"It is not my decision," Joshua said.

"Will you never stand and cry out to the Lord as Moses does?" Caleb strode into the courtyard of the Tabernacle. "*Lord!*" People stopped moving and stared. "Lord, send us." No one spoke or even dared breathe. "Deliver these people into our hands and we will destroy their cities!"

Moses rose from his knees and came toward him, face haggard. Caleb stood his ground. "Forty years we've wandered because we did not have the faith to go into the land. Will we lack faith again? The Lord said the land is ours. Don't tell me the Lord wants us to be attacked and made slaves again. I won't believe it!"

Moses' eyes caught fire. "The Lord has heard our plea

and given the Canaanites over to us. 'Go!' saith the Lord. 'Go and destroy them and their towns. Leave nothing stand-ing and no one breathing! Go in the name of the Lord.'"

And Caleb and Joshua did.

The place came to be known as Hormah: "Destruction."

+   +   +

When Moses led the community back toward the Red Sea in order to take the route around Edom, Caleb had to turn his mind to daily training rather than give in to his grow-ing tension and impatience to reach Canaan. When he heard grumbling, which came more often since the victory over the king of Arad, he reminded the people of what Moses had said: "The Edomites are sons of Esau, and therefore our brothers."

"Brothers who treat us like enemies!" Jesher was as eager to fight as his older half brothers Mesha and Mareshah.

"It matters not how they treat us." Caleb reined his sons in like young stallions. "We must do what is right."

"Anyone who stands in our way stands in the way of the Lord!"

Caleb felt a prickling of apprehension. He grasped Mesha by the shoulder. "Who are you to presume you know the will of God?" He dug his fingers in until his son winced. "It is Moses who speaks God's Word, and it is Moses who says we must go around Edom." He let go of his son and looked around the tent at the five others. "You would all do well to remember that, whether we like it or not, Esau's blood runs in our veins."

They couldn't quibble about Edom, so they focused their anger and impatience elsewhere.

"We never have enough water!"

"I'm sick to death of this manna."

"When will we have something else to eat?"

Beneath the surface of their complaints was a lusting for vengeance upon Edom and what they believed was a needless delay to the gratification of entering the Promised Land. The people coiled in small groups of malcontents, hissed and struck at Moses, forgetting how he had loved and prayed for them every day, all day, for forty years.

✦   ✦   ✦

Reaching for some firewood, Caleb felt a sharp sting. Sucking in his breath, he drew back his hand. A snake hung from his arm, fangs sunk deep into the tendons of Caleb's wrist. Pain licked through his veins. Some women screamed.

"Get back!" he cried out as he shook his arm. Rather than shaking free, the serpent's tail curled around his arm and tightened.

Caleb grasped the head and yanked the snake free, tossing it away from him. It coiled for another strike. Caleb's grandson Hebron drew his daggar and sliced off the snake's head. As its body writhed in the dust, Caleb crushed the head with his heel. Then, losing strength, he went to his knees.

The poison worked quickly. Caleb felt his heart pounding faster and faster. Sweat broke out and a wave of nausea gripped him. Someone held him gently and laid him down. "No," he rasped. "Get me up . . ."

"Father!" Mesha grasped him. Jesher and Mareshah came running, Shobab just behind them. They were all talking at once, no one listening. He saw fear in their eyes. Confusion.

"A snake bit him!" a woman sobbed. "It was in the wood. He—"

Vision blurring, Caleb grasped Mesha's belt. "Help me up . . ." He had to get to the Tabernacle. He had to see the pole with the replica of the poisonous snake attached to it. The Lord had promised that anyone who was bitten would live if he simply looked at it!

"Help him! Hurry!" Everyone cried out at once. His sons grabbed him by the arms and hauled him up. Mesha and Jesher supported him between them. He tried to walk, but his body betrayed him.

"He can't use his legs!"

"He's going to die!"

"Lift him!"

"*Hurry!*"

Four of his sons carried him, shouting as they wove their way through the tents. It seemed to take them forever. Were they so far from the Tabernacle?

"It's Caleb!" people cried out in alarm.

"Get back! Get out of our way!"

Caleb struggled for air. "Lord, You promised . . ." He could say no more.

"Father!" Mesha was crying.

I have come too far, Lord, to die now. You promised.

"Put him down!" someone said.

His sons lowered him to his knees, but he couldn't hold his head up. He couldn't breathe to tell his sons how to help him.

Oh, Lord, You know how many times we've broken our word to You, but You have never broken Your word to us. You said I would enter the land.

Caleb crumpled face-first into the dust. Hands fell

upon him again—so many hands, so many voices, shouting, crying.

Pray. Someone, pray.

"Caleb!" People surrounded them. "It's Caleb!" They
blocked the sun.

"Get back!" Joshua's voice this time. "Give him room
to breathe."

"Lord, Lord . . ." Caleb recognized Hur's voice, felt
himself being rolled onto his back. "Don't take him from
us, Lord."

Caleb lay on his back, the cloud above him, anguished
faces surrounding him. He couldn't raise his head. He
couldn't raise his hand to grab hold of someone and pull
himself up. His throat was closing, his lungs burning.

He felt Hebron lift his shoulders and prop him up, brac-
ing him. "Open your eyes, Grandfather. Look up. The pole
is right before you."

"Breathe, Father! Breathe!"

"He's dead!" someone shrieked. "Caleb's dead!"

People wailed.

With his last bit of strength, Caleb opened his eyes . . .
but he could see nothing. Darkness closed in around him.
"Look," Moses had said. "Look and believe and you will
live!" *You are my salvation, Lord. You alone.*

Spears of light came, driving the darkness back. His
vision cleared. Above him was the pole with the bronze
snake.

*You are the Lord. You are Rapha, the Healer. Your Word
is Truth.*

Caleb's lungs unlocked and he drew in a deep breath.
His heart slowed. His skin cooled. He came up through the
shadow of death, shaking off the fettering hands until he

was able to stand in the midst of the people. "Death, where is your sting?" he shouted.

His sons laughed in relief and thanksgiving.

Caleb raised his hands. "The Lord, He is God."

Shaken, tears in his eyes, Joshua cried out with him. *"The Lord, He is God!"*

Those surrounding them joined in shouting praises to the Lord, who kept His word.

✦　✦　✦

They moved from Oboth to Iye-abarim in the desert facing Moab toward the sunrise. Then they moved on to Zered Valley and farther to camp along the Arnon River on the border between Moab and the Amorites. The Lord led them to Beer and gave them water so they could cross the desert to Mattanah and on to Nahaliel, Bamoth and the Valley of Moab where the top of Mount Pisgah overlooked the wasteland.

Moses dispatched messengers to Sihon, king of the Amorites, requesting safe travel through his territory and also sent spies to Jazer. In response, Sihon mustered his entire army and marched out into the desert against Israel.

This time, the Lord sent them out. "Put the Amorites to the sword and take over his land from the Arnon to the Jabbok!"

At the blast of the shofar, Caleb raised his sword and let out a battle roar. Others joined in until the earth shook with the sound. Joshua led them into war. As they ran at the fortified city of Heshbon, Caleb shouted to his sons. "Destroy these people of Chemosh!" Chemosh, the false god who demanded the blood sacrifice of children.

The Israelite boys and young men Caleb and Joshua

had trained were now warriors eager to fight for the
Lord their God. They overran Heshbon, breaking down
its walls, smashing its idols and altars, and burning
everything that was left. They did not withhold their
hand, but cut down every citizen who remained to fight.
From Heshbon, they moved on to the surrounding settlements, clearing out the Amorites from their towns and
land. The vultures feasted.

Survivors fled along the road to Bashan and enlisted the
help of King Og, who marched his whole army out to meet
Israel at Edrei.

"Do not be afraid of them," Moses shouted. "Fear not,
for the Lord God has handed them over to you, Og and his
whole army and his land!"

When the day was over, not one Israelite had fallen, but
Og, his sons, and his entire army lay dead upon the field
of battle. Stained with blood, Caleb stood with his sons
among the twisted, tangled bodies of the slain. He heard
the jubilation of the men around him as they congratu-
lated one another on their victory. Did they really believe
their own strength had brought victory?

Caleb looked at the young men he had trained and
wanted to grab them by the throat. They now knew how
to fight, and they had the will to destroy. But they were
forgetting the most important lesson he had tried to drum
into their thick heads every day from the time they began
training: Love the Lord your God with all your heart,
mind, soul, and strength!

Panting, Caleb drove his spear deep into the earth that
now belonged to Israel. Thrusting his hands into the air,
he shouted with all his might, *"Lord! Lord! All praise to
the Lord!"*

His sons were the first to join in. One by one, others took up the cry until the sound swelled by thousands.

Make them remember, Lord. Write the truth upon their hearts.

✦   ✦   ✦

Israel camped on the plains of Moab along the Jordan across from Jericho. Caleb heard reports that Balak, king of Moab, was gathering forces and sending out messengers to Midian and other peoples of Canaan. "He intends to make an alliance with neighboring nations to keep us out."

"He won't succeed," Caleb vowed, pacing in front of his tent. He couldn't put his worry into words, and Joshua would wait upon Moses to make a decision. "I don't trust the Midianites. Something is wrong. I feel it."

"What?"

"They're too friendly."

"They are related to Moses' family."

Caleb knew as well as everyone else that Moses' wife Zipporah had been a Midianite, and her father, Jethro, had been a chieftain. When the Lord had brought the Israelites out of Egypt, Jethro had met Moses at the Mountain of God and returned to him Zipporah and Moses' two sons. Jethro had even advised Moses on selecting men from among the tribes to help him judge the birthing nation. A wise man, Jethro.

"Jethro was a man of honor, Joshua, but Jethro is long dead. Zipporah is not even a memory to these people, and Moses' sons are trained up in the ways of the Lord. They have nothing in common with their relatives who bow down to Baal."

"You judge them harshly, Caleb. Moses says to treat them as brothers."

"The women do not act like sisters. Have you sent anyone to see what's going on in Shittim?"

Joshua frowned. "No."

"Perhaps you should. Perhaps you should discuss these
concerns with Moses. Perhaps he should pray and ask God
why these Midianites are so friendly and if we should
have commerce with them." He had failed to keep the
impatience out of his voice.

Joshua glowered. "Moses is our leader. Not I."

"Does that mean you can't think for yourself?" Caleb
watched the color surge into Joshua's face and his eyes
darken. "Some of the men are leaving camp and going
over to the Midianite settlements. Did the Lord tell us to
mingle with these people? At one time, a long time ago,
Moses had reason to trust the Midianites. I am asking if
they are trustworthy now."

"If an opportunity arises, I will ask."

"Make the opportunity!"

Caleb left before he said harsher words. He called his
sons together and their sons. "You will not talk with the
Midianites or have anything to do with them."

"Has Moses ruled on the matter?"

Caleb turned to Ardon. "I have ruled on this matter,
and I am your father."

They had learned not to argue with him. No further
questions were asked.

But others training with Caleb's sons did as they
pleased, spending their leisure hours visiting with
Midianites. They brought back stories of how friendly and
how beautiful the young women of Midian were. Moses
had married one, after all. Was it any wonder they were so
attracted? And the feasting that went on beneath the

spreading oaks was unlike anything they had experienced in their desert life. Caleb came upon young men gathered tightly, whispering, laughing, eyes bright, cheeks flushed. "You should come and see for yourselves."

His sons wanted to go and pressed Caleb daily for permission.

"Everyone is going. We're the only ones who show such a lack of hospitality to Moses' relatives."

"You will not go over to them."

"Carmi lets his son go."

"And Salu."

"Salu is a Simeonite. You answer to me. And I say no. If you ask again, I will find work to keep you so tired you won't be able to stand, let alone think about Midianite women or their feasts!"

Despite Caleb's warning, some of the Judean men went to visit the Midianites. They didn't return until late. Several missed morning worship. One collapsed during training exercises. Caleb had no sympathy or patience. "Get your face out of the dirt."

The young man struggled to his feet, sallow, trembling, unable to look Caleb in the eye.

"Go back to your tent, Asriel." Caleb glowered in disgust. "Go! Now! Before I beat you into the ground!" He watched the young man stumble away. Turning to the others, he pointed after Asriel. "Can any man in that condition stand against the enemy? That is what happens when you stay out all night. You are worse than useless. You will cost the lives of your brothers! Never forget we serve the Lord, the God of Israel. And we are preparing to enter Canaan at His command. Our inheritance is over there." He stretched out his arm. "The Canaanites will not

throw open their gates to welcome us. Balak is building a
force against us. We do not have time to dance and sing
and feast with Midianites."

"The Lord has sent a plague upon us!" the people cried
out.

The people wailed, mourning the young men who were
dying. "Why?" a mother cried. "We have done everything God asked of us, and now He kills our children!
Why?"

✦   ✦   ✦

Asriel died. He was the first of many. None of Caleb's
sons were sick, but he questioned them anyway, pressing
until they told him what others had told them about the
Midianites and their comely young women and the feasts
that went on beneath the spreading oaks.

"No wonder God is killing us." Caleb wept. "We have
sinned against him." Caleb looked at Joshua, sitting beside
Moses, with the other elders gathered to discuss the
plague that was spreading through the camp. Hundreds
had died, and hundreds more fell ill every day.

"How have we sinned?" someone asked.

"The Midianites."

"They are our friends," another insisted.

"What friendship do we have with those who worship
idols? Remember Egypt!" Caleb had to remind himself that
the men gathered here had no recollection of what had
happened there other than what had been told to them.
They were the sons of those who had come out of slavery.
"The Moabites and Midianites know we belong to the God
who destroyed Egypt with plagues. They know we serve
Him. They are cunning enough to realize that they must

drive a wedge between us and the God we serve. So they send their beautiful young women to entice our young men into Baal worship. These women were sent to turn the hearts and minds of our sons away from God! And God is judging us for our unfaithfulness."

"I've seen nothing of that sort in our camp."

"Or ours!"

"Will we always be like this?" Caleb shouted, furious. Would they never understand? "Talking and talking. And still you fail to understand. God does not send a plague without cause. He does not punish without reason. We must examine ourselves so that we can repent!"

Moses leaned close to Joshua and spoke to him. Joshua nodded his head and whispered back. Agitated, others began talking at once.

"Salu," Caleb said loudly, "my sons tell me that your son Zimri visits the Midianites."

Salu the Simeonite looked less than pleased to be the center of attention. "He goes to tell them of our God."

"He brought a girl back with him," another added.

Moses' head came up. Joshua stared.

Salu shook his head. "No. You're wrong."

"I was on my way here when I saw your son with her," the man said. "I stopped him and asked what he was doing. He said he wanted all his friends to join him in a celebration, and this woman, Cozbi, had come to encourage us. He said she is the daughter of one of the Midianite chieftains. Zur, I think is his name."

"Invite his friends to a celebration?" Men looked at one another. "What did he mean by that?"

Abruptly, Phinehas rose and strode away from the gathering of elders. His father, Eleazar, high priest and son of Aaron, called after him. Phinehas didn't answer. He went into his tent and came out with a spear in his hand.

Caleb rose, staring after him. His heart raced. The son of the high priest looked neither to the right nor to the left as he strode toward the tents of Simeon. Caleb had never seen such an expression of wrath on a man's face, even in battle.

Moses' eyes went wide. At a word, Joshua was on his feet and following the high priest's son, Caleb right on his heels.

"What's the matter?" The others clamored to their feet. "What's happening?"

Phinehas broke into a run, spear high in his fist. He gave no battle cry as he charged. People scattered before him.

Caleb and Joshua ran after him, others falling in behind them. Among the tents of Simeon rose sounds of celebration. A circle of men and women stood around the entrance of a tent, staring, restless, moving, pressing in and leaning forward to see more.

"Get back!" At Joshua's shout, the people parted like a sea, exposing the debauchery that had so excited them. Some ducked their heads and ran, diving into their tents to hide themselves.

Phinehas entered the tent. With a loud cry, he planted his feet on either side of the couple writhing upon the mat, raised the spear in both hands, and brought it down with his full strength. The Midianite girl had seen him and screamed. Too late, she tried to kick back from beneath Salu's son, still in the throes of violent passion. Phinehas bore down on the spear, driving it through them both, pinning them to the ground. Salu's son died quickly, but Cozbi clawed and shoved, kicked and screamed, pressing

her heels until blood spilled from her mouth. Phinehas
held the spear until there was no movement, then let go
and backed away, gasping for breath.

Moses ordered the Israelite sons to stay away from the
Midianite camp. No further contact was to be made with
the Midianites. Eleazar made atonement for the people
who stood silent in fear of the plague. How many more
would die before the Lord took mercy upon them?

"From this day forth," Moses told the people, "treat the
Midianites as enemies. Kill them! They treated us as enemies." He called for a census. Twenty-four thousand had
died in the plague. Still, Israel's numbers had increased
since the first census before the Mountain of God.

Only two men remained from the generation of slaves
who had been delivered from Egypt: Joshua from the tribe
of Ephraim and Caleb of Judah.

+   +   +

"The Lord has called for vengeance on the Midianites!"
Moses told the people. "Arm one thousand men from each
tribe and send them into battle." Phinehas would lead
them into battle, taking with him the holy items and the
trumpets for signaling.

Whispers of alarm went through some ranks. Twelve
thousand against hundreds of thousands? They would be
slaughtered!

Faithless. Even now, faithless. "The Lord is with us!"
Caleb shouted.

"Fear no man!" Joshua called out, raising his sword.

After years of drilling and practicing, the young men
were eager to fight and prove themselves in battle. Everyone wanted to go. Caleb called for a lottery to eliminate all

but the one thousand men God would assign to fight for Judah. His sons were among them. They stood ready, dressed for battle, swords in hand, shielded by their faith in the living God they served. They had received the Lord's instructions. Now it remained to be seen if they would obey and receive the victory.

Caleb found himself left behind with the other leaders of the community, Joshua among them. Neither was at ease with the waiting.

Caleb heard the shofar blast in the distance and then the war cries of twelve thousand men going into battle. He longed to run with those men, to wield his sword, to kill God's enemies. But he waited with Joshua and the multitude. Let the younger men be tested.

Hour after hour passed. Moses prayed. Joshua prayed. Caleb tried, but his mind was in the midst of that battle, hands clenched, and sweat pouring. His sons had gone out to battle. His sons!

Don't let them fail, Lord. Hold them to their word. Keep their minds fixed upon You. Keep them faithful.

Forty years he had waited to enter the Promised Land. Forty years he had wandered with the sons of those who had refused to listen to his report about Canaan.

Messengers arrived. The Midianites had been conquered; the five kings—Evi, Rekem, Zur, Hur, and Reba— killed, as well as Balaam, King Balak's advisor. The men were returning in triumph.

Caleb noticed Moses' anger and joined Joshua and Eleazar, the high priest. "What's wrong?"

"The men are bringing back captives."

Fear gripped Caleb. Would the Lord send yet another plague upon them?

Herds of cattle and flocks of sheep and goats were being driven toward the camp, and Caleb could see carts of plunder and men carrying all manner of goods they had taken from the Midianite cities and villages.

"Why have you let all the women live?" Moses cried out against them. "These are the very ones who followed Balaam's advice and caused the people of Israel to rebel against the Lord at Mount Peor. They are the ones who caused the plague to strike the Lord's people. Now kill all the boys and all the women who have slept with a man. Only the young girls who are virgins may live; you may keep them for yourselves."

Those who had fought in the battle were commanded to remain outside of camp. They were to wash themselves and their clothing and everything made of leather, goat hair, or wood. All gold, silver, bronze, iron, tin, and lead were to be put through the fire. Every idol and item bearing the emblems and symbols of pagan gods would be melted down. The spoils were divided among the soldiers who had taken part in the battle and with the rest of the community. One out of every five hundred persons, cattle, donkeys, goats, and sheep was given as tribute for the Lord and placed in the care of the Levites.

Caleb's sons returned to their tents with their share of plunder. He stood as they approached, heat surging into his face, every muscle taut. Mesha and Mareshah stood before him with the confidence of soldiers who had returned from a great victory. And indeed it had been. Not one Israelite had fallen.

"We have brought you presents, Father."

"I asked for nothing." Nor did he want what they had brought back to him.

"You have not had the comfort of a woman since Jerioth and Ephrathah died."

"And you think I will take a Midianite as my wife? I am the one who told you to have no commerce with them!"

"These girls are no longer Midianite. They belong to us now. If you will not have them as wives, take them as concubines."

"They know nothing of who we are or what we've been through. Nor of the God we serve."

"Then teach them as you taught us," Mareshah said gravely.

Mesha stepped closer. "We must increase our numbers, Father. And you need women to accomplish that." He grasped one of the girls by the arm and yanked her forward. "She is young, healthy, and gave us no trouble. Do with her what you will." He pushed her forward.

The girl looked at Caleb with calf eyes. He could see nothing in her expression to give him any idea of what she was thinking. He thought of the young Midianite women laughing and beckoning to the men he had trained, leading them away like lambs to the slaughter. Twenty-four thousand had died because men had been easily seduced into Baal worship. The girl had slender curves and smooth olive skin. She would become a beautiful woman. He put his hand to his sword and drew it.

Though the girl's lips parted, she didn't speak. Closing her eyes, she knelt and bowed her head.

"It would be a waste to kill her, Father." Mesha made no move to stop him.

"Do you mock me?" Caleb was eighty years old.

"All those who called you a dog are dead. You are

respected by all who know you. And you are my father. You would have led us into battle if God had called you to do it!" Mesha said.

"Moses said we were to keep the virgins." Mareshah spoke quietly.

Hur stretched out his hand and drew another comely young woman forward. "You deserve the best of our portion." The second young woman knelt beside the first, trembling.

Mesha gripped Caleb's sword arm. "They are yours, Father. Make good use of them for all our sakes."

Left alone, Caleb stood over the two young women, sword in hand.

Judgment or mercy, Lord. What do I do?

He waited, longing for a word, a sign, from the Lord. He studied the two before him. One finally raised her head and looked at him. Her dark eyes shone with fear, but she did not beg for her life. The other girl, still trembling violently, began to sob.

Caleb thought of the countless times God had shown mercy to him and to the people. Was it only accident or circumstance that had plucked these two young women from their foul culture and placed them here in the midst of Israel? Or did God have a plan for them, too?

"I am Caleb." He put his hand over his heart. "Caleb."

The girl who was looking at him placed her hand over her heart. "Maacah." She touched the bowed head of her sobbing companion. "Ephah."

"Life and death are before you. If you learn the law of God and obey, you will live."

Maacah frowned, perplexed. She spread her hands and shook her head.

Caleb scowled. Of course she could not understand his language. But she must learn the most important thing, language barrier or not. "The Lord." He spoke firmly, with a nod of expectation. "The Lord!"

She understood. "The Lord." She spoke hesitantly, then drew up the girl beside her. She spoke to her. Then they both spoke together. "The Lord."

It was not enough to repeat what he said. They must understand he was not speaking of himself, but of the One they must learn to serve. Caleb stretched out his arm, pointing toward the Tabernacle, where the Ark of the Lord was hidden in the Holy of Holies. "The Lord. The Lord, *He is God!*"

Maacah's beautiful dark eyes widened. "The Lord." She spoke in awe. Her expression gave Caleb cause to hope. If these two young women learned that, they would have learned more than the people who had wandered and died in the wilderness.

"The Lord, He is God."

The two young women repeated Caleb's words.

Caleb sheathed his sword. He called to one of his granddaughters. He pointed at each of the young women his sons had given him and gave their names. "See that they learn our language. Then they will learn the law of God."

He would not have anything to do with them until they did.

FOUR

"WHEN you cross the Jordan River into the land of Canaan, you must drive out all the people living there."

Caleb stood in front of the tribe of Judah, listening to Moses give the Lord's instructions. This should be a day of exultation, but he felt weighed down. Forty years had passed. The wandering was over. And he was an eighty-year-old man. But it was not the years that burdened him. It was the responsibility for these people.

"You must destroy all their carved and molten images and demolish all their pagan shrines." Moses' voice carried. "Take possession of the land and settle in it, because I have given it to you to occupy. You must distribute the land among the clans."

Caleb had been placed in charge of all of Judah.

"If you fail to drive out the people who live in the land, those who remain will be like splinters in your eyes and thorns in your sides. They will harass you in the land where you live. And then the Lord will do to you what He plans to do to them!"

Time passed quickly as Moses reminded them of the plagues of Egypt and their own sins. "Hear, O Israel! The Lord is our God, the Lord alone. And you must love the Lord your God with all your heart, all your soul, and all your strength. And you must commit yourselves whole-heartedly to these commandments I am giving you today. Repeat them again and again to your children. Talk about them when you are at home and when you are away on a journey, when you are lying down and when you are getting up again. They are life to you. Make no treaties with the people of the land and show them no mercy. Do not intermarry with them."

Moses spread his hands as though he would embrace all of them. "I am now one hundred and twenty years old and am no longer able to lead you. The Lord has told me that I will not cross the Jordan River."

The people wailed and cried out in protest. Caleb clenched his teeth, tears spilled into his beard, his throat was tight and on fire. He looked at Joshua, standing tall beside Moses, his face set.

Moses raised his voice and through it came the voice of God. **The Lord your God Himself will cross over ahead of you!**

The people grew quiet again, grieving, yet obedient.

"The Lord will destroy the nations living there, and you will take possession of their land. Joshua is your new leader, and he will go with you, just as the Lord promised."

Eleazar the high priest anointed Joshua, after which Moses laid hands upon him and commissioned him to carry out the Lord's commands. Then raising his hands to the cloud overshadowing them, Moses sang Israel's history. He sang blessings upon them. And then he dismissed the congregation.

"He's gone." Joshua's voice was thick, fear glistening in his dark eyes.

"Gone where?"

"Up Mount Nebo." Joshua wept like a boy who had lost his father.

Caleb could not give in to tears, not if he was to be of any help to Joshua. "He will see the whole of the land God is giving us from there. He will see from Gilead to the Negev, from the Jordan Valley and Jericho as far as Zoar."

"I had hoped."

"We assumed Moses would be there, Joshua. We didn't understand that you and I would be the only men from our generation to enter Canaan."

"There will never be another prophet like Moses. No man will ever do the miraculous signs and wonders the Lord sent him to do in Egypt!"

"Until the One Moses said would come, the One who will fulfill the Law." But Caleb knew what lay beneath Joshua's words. "The Lord has appointed you to lead His people Israel. And lead you shall!"

Joshua put his hands over his head as though to hide from God. "I tremble at the thought."

"Fear of the Lord is the beginning of wisdom, my friend." Caleb sat down beside him. "When our time of grieving is over, God will tell you what to do. And whatever it is, I will stand with you."

✦   ✦   ✦

Caleb spent most of the day at the Tabernacle, close to Joshua, who was closeted in prayer. *Lord, help him. Be with him as You were with Moses. Tell him what he needs to know to lead us into our inheritance.*

They ate together in silence, pondering the days ahead, uncertain of how to proceed, where to start. For once, Caleb did not press his friend. He waited, knowing the day would come when the Lord would speak to Joshua as He had spoken to Moses.

Joshua rose and stood at the entrance of his tent. He stared out at Jericho looming on the other side of the Jordan, immense, fortified, a closed gate into Canaan. "Bring me two good men, Caleb." He spoke with an assurance

Caleb had not heard before. The Lord had spoken to him!
"Men other than your own sons. I'm sending them in to
look over the land, especially Jericho."

"Done."

When the young men had left on their errand, Caleb
tilted his head. "What else did the Lord say to you?"

"Be strong and courageous." Joshua smiled grimly. "He
said that many times."

"We all need to hear it." No man was eager to be in the
middle of a bloodbath.

"We must be very careful to obey all the laws Moses
gave us, Caleb. We must follow everything the Lord says."

Caleb knew Joshua meditated on the Law day and
night. "Anything else?"

"The Lord promised to be with me wherever I go."

Caleb's spirit rose like an eagle, wings spread. "Where
you are, there shall I be!"

"I need to speak with all the officers."

Caleb sent messengers and the men came quickly, ready
to do whatever Joshua told them. "Tell the people to get
their supplies ready. The Lord has said that three days
from now—" he pointed out the spot on the map Moses
had prepared—"we cross the Jordan here. We will take
possession of the land the Lord our God has given to us."

Even the Reubenites and Gadites, who had asked to
remain on the east side of the Jordan, prepared to go in and
fight for their brothers. "Whatever you have commanded
us, we will do, Joshua. Wherever you send us, we will go."

Everyone worked and prepared with practiced precision. The years in the wilderness, of watching the cloud
rise up, move, and settle, had trained the people to move
quickly when so commanded. The defeat of the kings

Sihon and Og encouraged them. Balak, king of Moab, had withdrawn now that Balaam and the five kings of Midian who had listened to his counsel were dead. Israel stood ready, eager to obey the Lord's command to take the land.

The spies returned with good news. "The Lord will certainly give us the whole land! Rahab told us the heart of every man in Jericho is terrified of us."

"Who is Rahab?"

"A prostitute." She had brought them into her house and made them swear by the Lord their God that they would save her and her family from the coming destruction.

Caleb's heart sank. Already, compromise. And then he thought of his two concubines and prayed, *Let this woman, Rabab, worship and adore You, Lord, as Maacah and Ephah have.*

"She protected us from the king's men and told us the way of escape. We might not have made it out alive without her."

Joshua asked no further questions. "Then you will see that you keep the vow you made in the name of the Lord. Gather the people tomorrow morning. I will give them the Lord's instructions."

As the men filed out of the tent, Caleb remained behind in case Joshua wanted to discuss plans and go over the maps again.

Joshua sat and beckoned him to do likewise. "We will cross the Jordan in two days. I didn't want to say anything to the officers. Not yet."

Caleb didn't have to ask why. The river was at flood stage, and no one in Israel knew how to swim or build rafts or a bridge. "I'm sure the Lord told you how we're to get across."

"No, He didn't. He only said the priests are to carry the Ark and the people are to follow a thousand feet behind."

Feeling a quiver of alarm, Caleb wondered what they would do once they reached the floodwaters. And then he remembered and laughed. "Do not be afraid, my friend! Do not be discouraged." He grinned. "A river is but a small matter to the God who opened a sea."

✦ ✦ ✦

"Gather around!" Caleb beckoned his sons and their wives and their children. They came eagerly. Ephah and Maacah were among his family members now, grafted in, warmly accepted, and held accountable to God. He told all of them of Egypt and slavery and how the Lord had sent Moses to deliver them. He told them of the plagues upon Egypt and about the miracles of protection God provided for His people. "You have heard your history from Moses' own lips, and you have heard it from mine as well. And so you will hear it often for as long as I live. And you must tell your children and your grandchildren so they will not forget."

Caleb reminded them of the sins committed that had brought God's judgment upon his generation. "Sin crouches like a lion waiting to devour you. You must resist it. You must obey the Lord. Do whatever He asks of you, no matter how difficult." He reminded them of the sins that had cost the lives of twenty-four thousand. "Your sins bring death to those you love. You must keep your eyes on the Lord. Not just tomorrow or until we have taken the land God has promised us, but *always*. Serve the Lord with gladness. Stand in His presence with thanksgiving! Our hope and our future are in Him."

His sons leaned in closer, eyes ablaze, tense. They had spent their lives preparing for the day at hand.

"Tomorrow you will hear the Word of the Lord from His anointed. Joshua will tell us what we are to do. Obey him as you would obey the Lord."

And thus they did.

The people consecrated themselves. They waited until the priests carrying the Ark were one thousand feet ahead of them and then followed. When the priests came to the Jordan River, they stepped down into it. A sound of wind came and the water rolled back, leaving dry land where water had rushed. The priests stood in the middle of the empty river-bed, holding the Ark, as men, women, children—over a million of them—crossed over. When the entire nation stood on the west bank of the Jordan, Joshua sent one man from each of the twelve tribes back, each for one river stone. He stacked them there at Gilgal on the eastern border of Jericho.

"In the future, your children will ask, 'What do these stones mean?' Then you can tell them, 'This is where the Israelites crossed the Jordan on dry ground.' For the Lord your God dried up the river right before your eyes, and He kept it dry until you were all across, just as He did at the Red Sea when He dried it up until we had all crossed over. He did this so that all the nations of the earth might know the power of the Lord, and that you might fear the Lord your God forever."

✦   ✦   ✦

"Joshua cannot have heard right, Father."

"The Lord commanded that we all be circumcised, and so we shall. I'm ashamed I did not think to do it years ago when you were boys."

"No one has been circumcised, not in forty years! We should wait."

"Wait?" Caleb glowered at his sons. "When God gives a command, we obey. We don't *wait*."

"Be reasonable, Father! We're camped within sight of Jericho. If we submit to this mutilation now, we won't be able to defend ourselves."

"Mutilation? You call the sign of the covenant between God and us a mutilation?" He watched the color drain from his son's face.

"I spoke rashly. Forgive me."

"It is God's forgiveness you need." He fixed his eyes upon each of his sons and grandsons. "Are you afraid of a small knife in the hands of a priest?" They all shook their heads, denying any fear.

Shobab laughed, self-deprecatingly. "*Yes*. I'm afraid."

"As am I," Caleb said.

"You?"

"Let it be a comfort to know that your father will be in line for circumcision tomorrow."

They all began talking at once. His words had not served to calm them, but caused even more agitation.

"Father . . ." Shobab pointed feebly. "Mesha is right. What is to keep the Canaanite warriors from coming out of Jericho and slaughtering us while we mend?"

"God has been with us every day, and you can ask such a question?" Restraining his anger, Caleb spoke slowly, quietly, empathically. "The Lord is our shield and strength. He will watch over and protect us. We have nothing to fear."

When the circumcisions were completed, Caleb retired to his tent. Racked with pain, he lay upon his pallet.

When fever came upon him, he couldn't sleep. Now that they had crossed the Jordan, the manna had stopped raining from heaven. His concubines, Ephah and Maacah, knew how to prepare meals from the provisions the land offered, but Caleb missed the manna. Gone was the sweetness God had given them.

Joshua came to see him. "Don't get up, Caleb."

Drained by the fever, Caleb remained upon his cushioned pallet. He chuckled bleakly. "You are blessed among men." Joshua had been circumcised as a baby. Few among the Jews had continued the practice once they were enslaved by the Egyptians. "How are the others faring?"

"Better than you, old friend."

Caleb grasped Joshua's extended hand and pulled himself up. "Youth has its advantages." Wincing, he waved Maacah away and walked . . . slowly . . . tenderly . . . outside. It was the first time in three days that he had been outside his tent. He squinted at the bright sunlight. "The Lord has given you His plan. When and how do we take Jericho?"

"Tomorrow at daybreak . . ." Joshua told him God's plan.

Astounded, Caleb went over the plan again. "We are to be silent?"

"Yes."

"No war cry."

"No one is to speak."

"And then we march around the city? Nothing more?"

"For six days. The Ark will go before us, followed by seven priests carrying shofars. On the seventh day, they will blow them and we will shout as we march around the city *seven* times."

Caleb looked at the walls of Jericho. Not since leaving Egypt had he seen such a well-fortified city. "And God said the walls will collapse?"

"Yes."

The plan was preposterous. It was ridiculous! No man in his right mind would ever have thought up such a thing. Caleb laughed in praise. "All the world will hear of this. People will talk about what God did at Jericho for thousands of years to come!"

"Then you believe it will happen?"

"Of course I believe it." Caleb's laughter died. "You don't?"

"Yes, *I* believe. But will the men?"

Caleb understood Joshua's trepidation. It had not been that long ago when some had gone after other gods at Peor. Twenty-four thousand had died during the plague God sent to discipline them. "They'd better."

From the time of the Garden of Eden, the seed of rebellion had been planted deep in the hearts of men. It was there the real battle raged.

✦   ✦   ✦

On the first day of marching, Caleb concentrated on putting one foot in front of the other. He throbbed with pain and gritted his teeth, determined to make it around the city and back to his tent with his head high. On the second day, he moved less stiffly and noticed the soldiers on Jericho's battlements staring out. On the third day, some mocked. By the fifth day, men and women were laughing and shouting blasphemies from the wall. Even children had joined in.

His sons and grandsons did not speak when they

returned to camp, but their wrath showed in the way they yanked off their belts and swords. Caleb watched them, smiling secretly, thanking God. The days of suffering from the circumcision were over. Each day renewed and built their strength. And each day the Canaanites added fuel to the fire that would consume them.

Let it build. Hold that anger in. Hold it in until the last day—the day of the Lord!

When the seventh day came, Caleb was at full strength, his blood on fire. The men no longer marched with quiet reserve. They pounded their feet into the ground. *Boom! Boom! Boom!* Each time around the city, the tension grew. The men on the walls of Jericho stopped laughing. Seven times the army of Israel marched around the city, shofars blowing. And then they stopped and turned inward.

The blast came—long and loud. Caleb's heart rattled; his blood raced. The air of retribution filled his lungs. He released it with a mighty shout. *"For the Lord!"* Thousands joined in until the sound was deafening, terrifying.

God's promise was fulfilled before their eyes. The great walls of Jericho shook with the sounds of the shofars and their battle cries. And as the walls shook and cracked, the Israelites shouted all the louder for the Lord. The walls collapsed, stones and rampart soldiers tumbling, dust rising with the screams.

Raising his sword high, Caleb ran with Joshua, and like a tidal wave, thousands upon thousands came with them, sweeping across the plain, straight for the city. The sword in his hand had once been a scythe, and he swung it to the right and left, cutting down Canaanites like stalks of wheat. Men, women, young and old, cattle, sheep, donkeys—nothing that breathed survived.

Panting, Caleb stood in the center of the vanquished city. "Remember your orders. All the silver, gold, bronze, and iron are sacred to the Lord and must be taken into His treasury. Destroy the rest! *Burn the city! Burn everything in it!*"

+   +   +

Jericho was still smoldering when Joshua sent spies to Ai, near Beth-aven. It lay to the east of Bethel, where Israel's ancestor Jacob had seen the ladder into heaven and the angels going up and down. The spies returned within a short time.

"It's not like Jericho. Not all our people will have to go up against it. Send two or three thousand men to take it. There's no need to tire the people over the few in Ai."

Joshua considered and then nodded. "Go and do so." As soon as the messenger left, Caleb leaned over the maps made from their first sojourn into Canaan forty years earlier. Joshua laid out God's plan to conquer Canaan.

+   +   +

"The men are returning from Ai." The breathless messenger looked ashen. "And they're bringing wounded and bodies!"

Caleb ran out to find his sons. Shobab was wounded. Mesha wept. "We thought it would be so easy after Jericho, but the men of Ai routed us! They chased us from the city gate as far as the stone quarries. The arrow hit Shobab while he retreated to the slopes. We ran!" He sobbed. "Ardon didn't make it, Father. He's dead!"

"My son? My son . . ." Caleb wept. How could this happen? How?

Joshua cried out at the news and tore his clothes. He went straight to the Tabernacle and fell facedown on the ground before the Ark of the Lord.

Caleb stood outside waiting, trembling. What had gone wrong?

The people began gathering—a dozen, a hundred, a thousand. Those who had lost sons and husbands wailed and threw dust over themselves.

Joshua came outside within moments, his face ashen. "We have violated the Lord's covenant."

Caleb felt cold. "When? How? Who?" Fear gripped him. What would God do to them? What plague would come upon Israel? What retribution for unfaithfulness?

"Someone has stolen things devoted to the Lord and then lied and put these things among their own possessions. Until this is settled, we can't stand against our enemies." Joshua's voice kept rising. "Consecrate yourselves!" he shouted to the people. "Present yourselves before the Lord tomorrow, tribe by tribe, clan by clan, family by family. The one who is caught with the devoted things will be burned, along with everything that belongs to him!"

Caleb gestured for his sons and grandsons, their wives and his concubines to return to their camp. He studied each one of his sons and grandsons. He looked at his concubines. He hated the feeling of distrust welling within him, the wrath and frustration, the fear of knowing someone who belonged to him may have brought God's wrath upon the entire nation. But who would dare steal from God? "God will tell us who the guilty man is. And whoever he is, he will die." *Don't let it be one of my sons or grandsons.*

No one said a word, but Caleb saw that his own feelings were reflected in their eyes. They looked at one another, questioning, wondering, afraid. Until the guilty party was found, everyone would be suspect.

No one slept that night. *Not one of my sons or grandsons, Lord. Let it not be anyone from Judah.*

In the morning, Eleazar the priest stood with Joshua as the tribes came forward one by one. The Reubenites passed by, then the Simeonites. Judah was halted. Caleb wanted to sink into the ground in shame. As the other tribes moved back from them, Judah came forward clan by clan. Caleb went first, followed by his sons, grandsons, and all their wives, concubines, and children. They were not stopped. But Caleb felt no great relief. *Judah, oh, Judah. Leader among your brothers! Are you leader in sin as well?* The Shelanite clan passed by, then the Perezites.

When the Zerahite clan came before Eleazar and Joshua, they were halted. Joshua commanded them to come forward by families.

Caleb watched Eleazar and knew the moment God revealed the guilty man: Achan, son of Carmi, son of Zimri. Caleb hung his head and wept. Achan and Ardon had played together. They had trained together, laughed together, gone out to battle together.

"It is true! I have sinned against the Lord, the God of Israel." Achan spoke quickly, pacing and sweating in fear before Joshua and Eleazar, turning to his Judean brothers. "I saw a beautiful robe imported from Babylon, two hundred silver coins, and a bar of gold weighing more than a pound. I wanted them so much that I took them. They are hidden in the ground beneath my tent, with the silver buried deeper than the rest."

"Go!" Joshua gestured to two assistants, and they departed. Everyone waited until they returned with the beautiful multicolored, woven, embroidered robe; the silver; and the gold. The silver and gold were given to Eleazar and the priests to spread out before the Lord.

Joshua turned to Caleb, his eyes filled with sorrow. "We must take Achan and all that belongs to him to the valley."

As head of Judah, Caleb obeyed the command. Achan did not go easily. "I'm sorry! I didn't mean to do it. I don't know what got into me! It's just a robe and some silver and gold. Is that reason enough to kill me and my entire family? Caleb, help me. My grandfather and father were your friends. The council will listen to you. *Help me!*"

Grief and disappointment fueled Caleb's rage as he backhanded Achan, who fell to his knees begging. Pity caught at Caleb, but he dragged him up. His son Ardon had died because of this man's sin. So had thirty-five others! Caleb thought of their widows and children as he propelled Achan ahead of him. He would not listen to Achan's excuses or his pleas for mercy. He closed his ears to the sobs of Achan's sons and daughters as others pressed them along after their father. Even the man's cattle, donkeys, and sheep were driven into the valley, and his tent and all he had were cast down around him.

"Spare my children!" Achan screamed, weeping. "At least my sons so that my name will . . ."

"Why have you brought trouble on us?" Joshua's voice carried so that all those standing around the rim of the small valley heard. "The Lord will now bring trouble on you." He took up a rock. Caleb did likewise, gripping it tightly, palm sweating, tears filling his eyes.

Achan's screams were abruptly silenced, as were those of his sons and daughters. The animals were not so easily killed. When everything that breathed was dead, the remains and all Achan's possessions were torched. Then stones were piled up in a heap.

Silent, the people dispersed.

Caleb returned to his tent with his sons and grandsons. Some wept. Others were quiet. Some questioned.

Caleb stood firm. "Achan had to die!"

"Yes, but did his children?" One of the women wept.

Caleb felt every day of his eighty years. "They knew. Don't you understand? They all knew. Achan buried inside his tent what he stole from God. Do you think his sons and daughters didn't know about it?" He swept his arms wide. "Could I dig a hole here and my family not see it? No! Achan's sons and daughters saw what he did and said nothing. They forsook the Word of the Lord and followed their father. They were all guilty!"

"He loved Ardon like a brother." Shobab shook his head. "They were friends from childhood. You heard what he said. He wasn't thinking clearly when he took those things. It all happened in the heat of battle. He didn't mean to sin . . ."

"*Do not pity him!*" Tears streamed down Caleb's face. "Achan knew he sinned. It took time to smuggle those things out of Jericho. It took time to hide them. He thought he could steal from God and no one would know, and Ardon died at Ai because of him. To show him pity is to rebel against the Lord's judgment. Think of Ardon and the thirty-five others who died because of one man's greed. We grieve and suffer now because of Achan. He had herds of cattle and flocks of sheep. His sons rode on donkeys like young princes. God had given him wealth. Was he satisfied? No! Was he thankful? No!" He spit in disgust. "Your brother and the others died because Achan wanted a robe, a few silver shekels, and a wedge of gold!"

For forty years, he had taught and counseled his sons and grandsons. Did they still not understand? "You *must* obey the Lord. Whatever He says, you must do. God gave us the Law to protect us, to teach us how to live righteously before Him. The battle belongs to the Lord. We are to be holy as He is holy!"

"How can we do that, Father?" Hur, the only son of his beloved Ephrathah, leaned forward. "You know we love you and respect you." He held his hands out. "We all strive to do whatever you ask of us because we know you live for God. But I want to know, Father. How is it possible to be holy like God? How can we keep every law laid upon our backs? I try. God must know I try. But I fail."

Caleb saw the anguish in his son's eyes. He saw the others were troubled as well.

"Yes." He let out his breath slowly. "Yes, we all fail." He banged his chest with his fists. "But inside, we fight to do what the Lord wills. We must fight our inclinations!" They listened more intently now than they had for a long time. "The battle is not over what's out there. The battle is within us, always within us."

Achan had been judged rightly, and now they must forget their sorrow and their losses and move forward. With God!

"If you can only remember one command, my sons, let it be this: Love the Lord with all your heart, mind, soul, and strength. If you can do that, God will show you that all things are possible with Him." Caleb spread his hands.

"Say it with me." And they did. "Say it again." And they did, louder. "*And again!*" And they shouted it.

"Say it every day for the rest of your lives, and live by your word." Bowing his head, Caleb prayed a blessing upon them.

✦   ✦   ✦

"Hide in ambush close behind the city and be ready for action." Joshua pointed to the map. Caleb studied the markings so he would know where he would hold the men. Joshua straightened. "When our main army attacks, the men of Ai will come out to fight as they did before, and we will run away from them. We will let them chase us until they have all left the city. For they will say, 'The Israelites are running away from us as they did before.' Then you will jump up from your ambush and take possession of the city, for the Lord your God will give it to you."

"And when we have the city in our hands?"

"Set the city on fire, as the Lord has commanded. You have your orders."

Caleb led the men by night to their position behind the city. They waited until early the next morning when a messenger reported that Joshua had mustered his men and was on the move. From his position, Caleb could see Joshua's army approach the city and form in front of it, setting up camp north of Ai, with a valley between them and the city. With Caleb's five thousand men to the west of the city, the men of Ai would be boxed into that valley with no escape.

Shouting arose as warriors poured from the gates of Ai, chasing Joshua and his army toward the desert. Caleb snapped his fingers and several messengers ducked down beside him. "The men of Ai are in pursuit of Joshua. Alert the men!" The men of Ai raced across the valley, leaving the gates of the city open and unguarded. Spotting Joshua, Caleb waited, teeth gritted, for the sign.

And then it came. Joshua pointed his javelin toward Ai.

"Now!" Caleb shouted and rose up. Those under his command followed him up the slope and in through the city gates. People screamed and ran, but didn't get far. "Torch the city. Hurry!" Fires were set and the buildings took flame, smoke billowing into the sky. "To the battle!"

Caleb mustered his men. The warriors of Ai were in full retreat into the valley, but they couldn't escape for five thousand Israelites blocked them. "*For the Lord!*" Sword raised, Caleb ran toward the warriors of Ai. "For the Lord!" Thousands responded.

The valley became like a bowl of blood. Every warrior of Ai died there. Joshua took the king of Ai and hung him on a tree until evening, then ordered his body taken down and thrown on the burning city gate.

They built two altars of uncut stones, one on Mount Ebal and another Mount Gerizim. "Gather the people." When all the men, women, children, and aliens living among them were brought near, Joshua read the law God had given Moses to write. Not a word was left out.

The blessings and the curses were heard clearly from one mountain to the other. No one would ever be able to say they had not heard the Lord's warnings of what would happen if men failed to obey Him.

✦   ✦   ✦

"Who are you?" Caleb narrowed his eyes as he studied the ragged delegation of men, their donkeys loaded with worn-out sacks and cracked and mended wineskins. "Where did you come from?" A long distance from their appearance, for their sandals were patched.

"We are your servants. We have come to make a treaty with you."

Some of the younger men had gathered around to watch. "They might live near us. How can we make a treaty with them?"

Eleazar raised his hands. "Let them speak!"

Joshua looked them over. "Who are you and where do you come from?"

"We are your servants. We have come from a distant country because of the fame of the Lord your God. We heard reports about Him and all that He did in Egypt, and what He did to the two kings of the Amorites east of the Jordan, Sihon and Og. Our elders told us to take provisions and come and meet with you." The speaker reached into his pack.

Caleb drew his sword. A dozen others did the same.

The man's eyes went wide. "I only want to show you what has become of our provisions."

"Back away." Caleb stepped forward and looked in the pack.

"That bread was warm and fresh when we left our home." The man put his hand on the wineskins. "And these new and filled."

Caleb tore off a piece of bread. After a taste, he spit it out. "Dry. Moldy." But he still didn't trust them.

"We'll make a treaty with you."

Joshua and most of the elders were in agreement.

Caleb was not so easily convinced. "The Lord said to make no treaties."

"Yes." Joshua grew impatient. "But we must not be too quick to judge and wipe out people. The Lord meant no treaties with those of the land. These men are from a distant country. We have no reason to be at war with them."

"Then why do I feel this unease in my gut?"

Joshua slapped him on the back. "Perhaps it is the bread you just ate."

Others laughed, friends of old. Overruled, Caleb kept silent.

The delegation left soon after the treaty was made. Three days later, Israelite warriors sent to scout out the land returned, red-faced and raging. "They're Hivites from Gibeon! Those clothes they wore were a ruse. We did not attack because we signed a treaty with them."

Caleb exploded in anger. "They made fools of us!"

"Of me." Joshua was pale with mortification. "I did not inquire of the Lord. I did what I thought was right."

"Well, you had better pray now, my brother, because we are in trouble. The people are not happy about what we've done."

The people grumbled. "God said not to make a treaty with these people!"

"What were you thinking?"

"They'll be a thorn in our sides from now on!"

The leaders argued among themselves over what to do. "*They lied!*"

"We don't owe them anything!"

The tribe of Simeon was eager for blood. "I say we march on their cities and kill every last one of them!"

Those representing the other tribes were as eager for revenge. "That's what the Lord told us to do in the first place."

Joshua shook his head. "We must keep our oath."

Caleb listened to the others all talk at once. They were afraid, and with good reason. The people were angry and casting blame. "Be still!" He spoke loudly, and the others quieted. "We made a mistake in not asking God who those men were. We must not make another. My heart cries out for vengeance just as yours does, but vengeance belongs to the Lord. Listen to Joshua!"

They waited for God's chosen to speak.

"We have given them our oath by the Lord, the God of Israel, and we cannot touch them now. If we break our oath, we will bring God's wrath down upon us."

"So what do we do about them?"

Joshua called the people to order and told them the way of the Lord.

And then he summoned the Gibeonites. "Why did you lie to us?"

"We did it because we were told that the Lord your God instructed his servant Moses to conquer this entire land and destroy all the people living in it. So we feared for our lives because of you. That is why we have done it. Now we are at your mercy—do whatever you think is right."

Whatever you think is right. Caleb seethed. These people knew the oath could not be broken without incurring God's wrath. The Gibeonites had counted on it.

The people grumbled. A wave of fury could be felt until Joshua reminded them that the Lord would hold the nation to their oath. He faced the frightened Gibeonites. "You are under a curse. From this day forth, you will never cease to serve as woodcutters and water carriers for the house of my God." They bowed before him and departed.

The camp was quiet that night.

God's enemies would now retain a toehold in the land for generations to come.

✦   ✦   ✦

Summoned by messenger, Caleb hurried to Joshua's tent. One look at Joshua's face and Caleb knew something was wrong. "What's happened?"

"The Gibeonites have sent word they need our help. The Amorite kings of Jerusalem, Kiriath-arba, Jarmuth, Lachish, and Eglon have moved against them."

"It's bad enough that we have to allow those people to live. Now we have to defend them?"

They gathered the entire Israelite army and marched all night to rescue Gibeon. In the morning they took the attacking armies by surprise.

"Look," Caleb cried out. "The Lord is with us!" The enemy was in confusion, bumping into one another in their haste to flee. The battle raged.

"Joshua! Joshua!" A young warrior panted before him. "The kings! I saw all five of them go into a cave."

"Roll large rocks up to the mouth of it and post guards. Don't stop fighting! Pursue your enemies. Attack them and don't let them reach their cities."

Frustrated, Caleb assessed the numbers and the lay of the land. There were not enough hours in the day to complete the work God had given them. He sought out Joshua, who stood on the highest hill overlooking the battle, and voiced his concern. "We won't have the time to finish them. The sun is already overhead!"

Joshua shared his agitation. "We need more time! More time!" He raised his hands and cried out in a loud voice,

"Let the sun stand still over Gibeon, Lord, and the moon over the valley of Aijalon!"

They joined the battle. As Caleb swung his sword from the right to the left, Amorites fell before him like stalks of wheat before a reaper. He kept on, cutting down any man who came against him, until he could no longer number those he had killed. His arm did not weaken, and the sun seemed to remain overhead! But how could this be? Hour after hour, the sun remained in the middle of the sky, blazing down upon the battlefield.

"The Lord! The Lord, He is with us!" Exultant, Caleb let the fire within him blaze. Surely all the nations would see that the Lord God of Israel had power not only over all creation but over time itself. No one could fight against God and win!

The Amorites fled, and Caleb and Joshua raised their swords. "After them!"

The Israelites pursued the enemy up to Beth-horon, but before they caught up with them, the Lord cast hailstones the size of a man's fist from heaven. Caleb saw men struck in the head and back, crashing to the ground. Battered and bloody bodies lay along the road. So many were strewn along the way that Caleb knew the Lord had killed more by hail than he and the others had killed by the sword.

The army camped at Makkedah, and reports began coming in from the captains. "The Amorites were destroyed. Only a few managed to make it to their cities."

Thankful that God had given them one more full day of sunlight during which to fight, Caleb was still not satisfied with the outcome. "And those few who escaped will be a thorn in our side if we don't hunt them down and destroy them."

"We have the kings in the caves," Joshua reminded him.

The order was given to open the cave and bring the kings out. When a contingent obeyed, the kings appeared, blinking at the bright sunlight. For all their grand apparel and lofty plans to annihilate Israel, they were thrown to the ground before Joshua. He called for the commanders to come forward. "Put your feet on the necks of these kings."

Caleb motioned for Mesha to put his foot on the neck of Adoni-zedek, king of Jerusalem.

"Do not fear these men." Joshua drew his sword. "They fled the battle and hid in this cave." One by one, he struck and killed them. "Hang them on the trees until evening," he ordered. "Then throw their bodies into the cave. Tomorrow we take Makkedah!"

Swords were raised, and the sound of triumph rang.

But Caleb wondered why nothing much was said about what the Lord had done for them that day. Joshua could talk of little else, and Caleb's own heart sang praises. But what of the younger men, the captains and those in their charge? God had provided the people with manna and water in the desert for forty years. In all that time, their clothes and shoes had not worn out. God's presence and protection had been with them in the cloud and pillar of fire. Had they all become so accustomed to miracles that the Lord's stopping the sun seemed a small matter?

Caleb wondered about the days ahead. Victory sang in the air. The Promised Land smelled sweet with the blossoms of fruit trees, fields of grain, vineyards, and olive trees. But was taking the land their only goal?

Lord, don't let us become complacent. Don't let us become so used to miracles that we fail to recognize and give thanks and praise for what You do for us. Sometimes You are so vast, Your ways so incomprehensible, that we fail to see You at all. And You are here. You are over us and behind us. You go before us and are our rear guard. You breathe life into us.

Let us never forget that we are but dust without You, only chaff to be blown away by the lightest breeze that may come against us.

✦   ✦   ✦

Makkedah fell and the Israelites left no survivors. Libnah, Lachish, Eglon, Kiriath-arba, and Kiriath-sepher met the same fate. The Lord's command to destroy all who breathed was carried out. But some fled to the north and to the coastlines.

The Amorites, Hittites, Perizzites, Jebusites and Hivites joined forces at the Waters of Merom.

"They have a huge army!" The scout's eyes were dark with worry. "And thousands of horses and chariots. There are too many for us . . ."

"How many is too many for the Lord, Parnach?" Caleb drew the tent flap back. "You're dismissed."

The young man flushed and departed quickly.

"Perhaps we should rethink our battle plan," said Joshua.

Our battle plan? Joshua looked tired. So were they all. They had been fighting for months, taking one city after another, putting thousands to the sword. "We never fight by *our* battle plan, Joshua. You know that better than any man. Inquire of the Lord. He will tell you again what we must do."

"How many times must the Lord say to me, 'Have no fear' before I have no fear?"

Caleb frowned. "You are not a coward, Joshua."

Joshua gave a grim laugh. "The Lord knows differently."

"If you are a coward, so are we all. Not a man among us is without fear, my friend. Brave men do what the Lord commands despite their fear. As you have done, and so shall the Lord tell you to do again."

"You are the fiercest man I've ever known, Caleb. I've never seen you waver, even when cutting down women and children."

"Because I fear God more than men. But I am sick after every battle."

"I find that hard to believe."

"Ask Maacah. Ask Ephrah." Killing women and children was a difficult thing to do. "I must remind myself continually of what I saw during those forty days we traveled through this land as scouts. Remember their festivals, the debauchery, the perversion, the way they sacrificed their children to their gods? Even the children acted out what they saw their parents doing. We told them the stories of our God, how He destroyed Egypt with plagues, how He provides for His people. Have they changed? When we went into Jericho, what did we find but altars like those we saw all over Canaan. Rahab said the people were afraid of us, but do they fear God? No! Forty years, Joshua. The Lord is merciful to those who repent and cry out to Him. Have these people done that?"

Caleb clenched his fist. "I have to remind myself of these things every time I draw my sword. I have to remind myself of what God requires of me. We all must remind ourselves that God is on our side. As long as we obey His Word, He will protect us and give us the victory. As long as we obey."

"That preys upon my mind. How long will our people obey? We have seen that their hearts are easily seduced."

"And that is precisely why the Lord told us to get rid of these people, to be a scourge and cleanse the land of them. We erred with the Gibeonites, Joshua. We must never make that mistake again."

Joshua's eyes shone. "We won't. Not as long as I live. I will inquire of the Lord and we will follow Him."

Caleb smiled.

"There is momentum in these battles, Caleb, like a great stone rolling down a mountain. The Canaanites, Amorites, and all the rest flee before us because God hardened their hearts. Their opportunity to repent has passed. And God is using us to carry out His judgment against them."

"Yes, Joshua, but we must not forget that we could share the same fate if we ever turn our backs on the Lord."

God had told them He would bring the curses to bear upon them and they would be cut down by the sword and scattered across the face of the earth.

✦   ✦   ✦

"*For the Lord!*" Caleb led Judah's charge into battle at the Waters of Merom. Joshua was at the head of Israel's divisions. The army of Amorites, Hittites, Perizzites, Jebusites, and Hivites fell before the ferocity as the Lord gave them into the hand of Israel. The allies split, retreating.

Caleb cut down all those who stood against him. His arm swung to the right and then the left, hacking through any Amorite or Hittite who came at him. He saw others run. "Pursue them!" he shouted and the Hebrews went after them.

Bodies lay all along the way to Greater Sidon, to

Misrephoth-maim and to the Valley of Mizpah on the east. Hamstrung horses screamed. Chariots burned. One by one, cities fell. The Israelites followed the command to leave no survivors. They left the uninhabited dwellings and cities on their mounds and moved on to Hazor and King Jabin, the man who had gathered the other nations against Israel. And the city fell.

"Here he is!" Caleb threw King Jabin at Joshua's feet. When the Amorite king tried to rise, Caleb put his foot on his back.

"We wait—" Joshua drew his sword—"until every man, woman, and child in his domain has reaped the Lord's wrath."

When the city was silent, Joshua drew his sword. "For the Lord." He sliced through Jabin with one powerful sweep of the blade. Caleb stood near enough to be splattered by the blood as the Amorite king died.

The men cheered in victory.

"Hazor has well-built walls, fine dwellings, and cisterns."

Caleb knew what they were thinking. After years of living in tents, how easy it would be to move into those houses and live in comfort. Hadn't he been tempted by the same things? But there were other things to consider. "There is an altar to Baal at the center and an Asherah pole. I did not enter a single household where there was not some kind of idol."

The officer from Simeon glared at Caleb. "We can put everything through fire as we have before."

Cattle lowed and sheep bleated as they were herded toward the valley. Israel's flocks and herds were growing with every battle they fought. Even in their dreams, they had not imagined the wealth God had given them.

Caleb thought of the blood on the altar in the center of Hazor. "What does the Lord say about *this* city?"

Joshua walked away from them. When one of the men started to follow, Caleb blocked him. "Let him inquire of the Lord."

The commanders all talked at once. What they wanted was clear.

Caleb stilled his impatience. "Jabin gathered the nations against us."

"Jabin is dead!"

"Yes, I know he is dead. And Hazor stands as a monument to his rebellion."

"We'll rename the city. We can burn all the idols and smash the Asherah pole and the altars of Baal."

"Should we bring our children to live in a city founded upon sin?"

"You would tear down every one of these towns, Caleb. You are a destroyer!"

"I saw what they did on those altars. In forty years, I have not forgotten."

"We didn't see it, Caleb. We aren't plagued by such memories. We can—"

"Be silent!" Caleb commanded. Joshua was returning. "What does the Lord want done, Joshua?"

Joshua came toward them, wrath in his eyes. "Burn it. The Lord says burn it. *Leave nothing standing!*"

Caleb called out the order. Men ran to obey, tearing down the gates and setting a torch to them. The crackle of flames filled the air along with billowing smoke. Caleb strode through the city, making certain the dwellings were set on fire. He shouted to several men and ordered them to help him topple an Asherah pole. The stench of burning flesh filled his nostrils until he was nauseated.

As he went out, he drew in fresh air and thanked God for leading them away from temptation. Hazor had been a place of death long before God's wrath brought the Israelites to the gates of the city.

✦　✦　✦

Caleb cleaned the blood from his sword, then began the slow work of sharpening it. How many men had he killed in the last three years? How many more would he have to kill before God's enemies were removed from Canaan? He ran the stone along the blade in one long smooth stroke. He had met with Joshua last night and come away grim with resolve.

"The Lord has told me there are still large areas of land to be taken over," Joshua had said.

"What areas?"

"All the regions of the Philistines and Gershurites; from the Shihor River on the east of Egypt to the territory of Ekron on the north."

"Gaza and Ashdod?"

"Yes, and Ashkelon and Gath as well. From the south, all the land of the Canaanites, from Mearah of the Sidonians as far as Aphek where the Amorites still live, the area of the Gebalites; and all Lebanon to the east, from Baal-gad below Mount Hermon to Lebo-hamath."

The years stretched before Caleb. Would he ever plow the soil or plant seed again? Would he watch his crops grow? He couldn't speak.

Joshua pointed as he spoke.

"The Lord Himself will drive the Sidonians out of the

mountain regions from Lebanan to Misrephoth-maim. This
land will be allocated as an inheritance and divided among
the nine tribes and the half tribe of Manasseh."

Even as the fighting continued, the Israelites took possession of Canaan, dividing up the land according to the
boundaries set by the Lord. The Reubenites and Gadites
had received their inheritance, their clans and families
establishing themselves in the area taken from Sihon and
Og. The tribe of Reuben held the towns of the plateau and
the area once ruled by Amorites at Heshbon. The boundary was the Jordan River.

Gad received all the towns of Gilead and half the
Ammonite country as far as Aroer near Rabbah. Their territory ran up to the end of the Sea of Galilee. Manasseh's
territory included Bashan and all the settlements of Jair.
Sixty towns!

God assigned the other inheritances, and the areas were
marked out on a map. Judah's allotment was in the heart
of Canaan, including the mountain where Abraham had
taken Isaac and made ready to offer him to the Lord in
obedience to God's command, but the Lord had called out
to him to withhold his hand from the boy and provided
the offering Himself.

"Are you all right, Caleb?"

"I'm growing old."

Joshua's face softened. "Our day will come, my friend."

"Will it?" Caleb bowed his head in shame. Who was he
to question God? *Forgive me, Lord. It's only that* . . . He
stopped the thought. *Forgive me!* He fought against the
despair filling him. He had spent forty years wandering in
the wilderness because of the faithlessness of his generation. And now he was spending his last years fighting a

war and allotting the land to the sons of the very men whose sin had kept him out of the Promised Land all those years. The Lord would keep His promises, but that did not mean all would be as Caleb had hoped.

Canaan was a land of mountains and valleys, pasturelands and rippling streams. Blossoms scented the air and hummed with the bees that made honey, as cattle and sheep and goats on a thousand hills grazed and grew fat, providing milk and meat in plenty. The olive trees were loaded with their fruit, as were the apricot, pomegranate, and palm trees. Grapevines spread plentifully across the ground, bearing clusters enough to feed an entire family. The land of milk and honey!

Everything the Lord had said came true. The richness of Canaan made Caleb's head spin with dreams and longings he knew he must not dwell upon, for the Lord had not released him from his call to stand at Joshua's side. He must continue to wage war against the idol worshipers who had polluted the paradise God had created.

He must not question.

But sometimes the ache in his heart seemed past enduring. *Lord, Lord, help me!*

"The Lord will keep His promise, Caleb."

"He already has. The Lord promised that I would enter Canaan. And He has kept that promise." He looked away so that Joshua would not see the moisture growing in his eyes. Dropping his chin, he cleared his throat softly and waited a moment more before he could trust his voice. "God did not say I would return to farming."

FIVE

"WHEN do we get *our* land, Father? How long do we have to fight and place others first before we get our own inheritance?"

Caleb had struggled with these same questions over the past year. It wouldn't do to join in his sons' yearning. Joshua had not released him yet. "Our opportunity will come."

"*When?*"

"When Joshua says it is time."

"Joshua will never say it's time, Father. He needs you!"

"Do not speak as a fool. Joshua doesn't *need* me. The Lord is with him."

"He will never release you, Father. Not until you ask him to let you go."

Was that what they thought? "Joshua and I stood together against the unfaithful generation. We stand together now. He speaks for the Lord." Frowning, he watched his son Hur pour himself another cup of wine. Perhaps it was too much wine that roused their impatience this day. "My sons . . ." Caleb spoke gently, hoping to snuff out the sparks that could so easily take flame. "We may be twelve tribes, but remember, we are all sons of Jacob. We must work together to take the land. Together, we are strong in the Lord. Divided, we weaken."

"Yes." A young voice spoke boldly. "We must wait upon the Lord."

"Hush, Hebron!" Jesher glowered. "Who are you to remind us of the Lord?"

Hebron's face reddened, but he was wise enough not

to pursue the argument. Caleb studied his young grandson. At least one among these young lions had a heart for God. "Hebron speaks wisely."

"Hebron speaks as a boy with his whole life ahead of him." Jesher's eyes flashed. "What of you, Father?"

"Ah. So you cry out for my sake?" He mocked them. "Is it a cave you hope to claim? A place to put my bones?"

"We have waited long enough!" The others called out agreement.

"Manasseh, the Reubenites, and the Gadites haven't cleared their land of the enemy. When they do—"

"When they do?" Mesha rose, impatient. "They never will."

Caleb's face went hot. "Do not speak ill of your brothers." As each year passed, his own impatience grew. He did not need his sons to fan the blaze of sin.

"I speak the truth, Father, and well you know it."

His other sons joined in the argument. "Those tribes are not eager to aid us."

"They gave their word," Caleb reminded them in a hard voice. "And God will hold them to it."

"They long to return to their flocks and herds on the east side of the Jordan."

"If Moses hadn't made them take an oath, they wouldn't be helping us now. And they took that oath because they knew they'd all die if they didn't."

"They're half-minded, looking east rather than fully committed to the battle before us."

"Judah is like a lion, and you are the greatest lion of all, Father. Why must we be the last tribe to receive an inheritance?"

"*Enough!*" His sons fell silent before his anger. Caleb

clenched his teeth, and breathed out slowly before speaking again. "You call me a lion, and so I must rule this pride. *Listen. All of you!*" He waited for their full attention and spoke slowly, fervently. "We must encourage the others to fulfill the Word of the Lord. We must clear the land of every pagan. If we fail in this, the Canaanites, Amorites, Hittites, and all the rest will be stumbling blocks for generations to come!"

"We will drive them from our land, Father. We will kill them!"

"It is these other tribes who do not seem intent on getting the work done." Mesha leaned toward Caleb, eyes hot. "If we wait, we will have nothing!"

Caleb grabbed Mesha by the throat. Mesha grabbed his wrist, but could not break free. Caleb dug his fingers in until Mesha's eyes rolled back, then let him go. Mesha rasped, coughed.

"If you ever speak rebellion against the Lord again, I'll kill you." Caleb turned his face from Mesha and looked at each of his sons, one at a time. "Don't make the mistake of thinking I'll spare my own household!"

There was silence in the tent. No one moved. Not even the women standing by, ready to serve.

Shobab, ever the peacemaker, spread his hands in a conciliatory gesture. "We ask only that you pray about it, Father. Your heart is pure before the Lord."

"Pure?" Caleb sneered. "No man has a pure heart." Not even Joshua could boast such a thing. Caleb exhaled slowly. They were so quick to battle. Should any man take pleasure in shedding the blood of an enemy? No! Did God take pleasure in killing? Never! Caleb could not help wondering if there would come another day when Israel would be an enemy of God and the judgment would come upon

them. These sons of his had only been in the Promised
Land four years, and already the bones left in the wilderness were forgotten.

I will not forget, Lord!

He would not allow himself to believe he was impervi-
ous to sin, that it could not draw him into deceit and bring
him down as it had brought down other men better than
he. Moses, for one.

"I have prayed, Shobab. I continue to pray. I see what
you all see, and long for our land as much as—if not more
than—you do. But we *must* wait upon the Lord! We *must*
do all according to God's plan and not our own. If we go
after what we want now, we are even less than these
brothers you speak against. Without the Lord on our side,
we have no hope or future."

Caleb felt compassion within his anger. Some of these
sons were now older than he had been when he first set
foot in Canaan forty-four years ago. They saw the land as
he had then, a fulfillment of God's promise, a place of milk
and honey. But it was also a place that ran deep with the
corruption of the people who had dwelt upon it. The land
must be cleansed first, and then it would become what
God meant it to be: a land and people ruled by the God of
heaven and earth. And all the nations of the earth would
see the difference between His ways and those of men.

These sons, so much like him, thought only of land and
houses, a place to rest. Surely God's plan was greater than
to sit beneath an olive tree and enjoy the fruit of the land.
Caleb was convinced God's plan was greater than any man
could imagine. Judah was like a pride of lions. And Caleb
must be the strongest lion among them. He must do battle
against them for their sake.

"I did not wander for forty years in the wilderness and oversee your training so that we would become like a pack of wolves, thinking only of ourselves!" Caleb raised his fist. "We shall lead the other tribes as God bids us lead them. Let them see Judah wait. Let them see Judah fight so that others might claim their inheritance first."

Reaching out, he rested his hand gently on Mesha's shoulder. "Let them see this pride of lions show humility."

✦   ✦   ✦

Caleb dreamed again of the hill country. Hunkering down, he took a handful of soil and rubbed it between his fingers, letting it sift and drop. Above him was Kiriath-arba with its high gates and fierce warriors.

Let me have them, Lord. Let me vanquish them.

Go, My servant. Take the land.

Startled awake, Caleb sat up. His heart drummed. A strange prickling sensation made every hair on his body stand up. "Lord," he whispered. "So be it." He stood, dressed, and called for his servant. "Rouse my sons and tell them to gather Judah."

The men came and stood waiting for his instructions. "We go to Gilgal." He did not have to say more. The men cheered.

Caleb led the sons of Judah up the hill. One of the men standing before Joshua's tent ducked inside. Joshua came out. He moved toward Caleb, and clasped arms with him. He looked past him to the men and then released Caleb. "Speak, my friend. Why have you come?"

"Remember what the Lord said to Moses, the man of God, about you and me when we were at Kadesh-barnea. I was forty years old when Moses, the servant of the Lord,

sent me from Kadesh-barnea to explore the land of Canaan.
I returned and gave from my heart a good report, but my
brothers who went with me frightened the people and discouraged them from entering the Promised Land. For my
part, I followed the Lord my God completely. So that day
Moses promised me, 'The land of Canaan on which you
were just walking will be your special possession and that
of your descendants forever, because you wholeheartedly
followed the Lord my God.'"

Joshua nodded gravely. "I remember well."

Caleb, too, remembered. The memories came with a
rush of sorrow. They had been bound together because of
their faith, two men against a nation. Had God not stood as
a wall between them and the sons of Israel, he and Joshua
would have been stoned to death. He remembered the
forty days of traveling with Joshua, how they had entered
the towns and pretended to be traders, how they had
talked to the people of the land, telling them of the
plagues of Egypt, the Red Sea opening, the cloud and pillar of fire that sheltered them. They had given warning.
None had listened.

Joshua had been a young man then, untried, eager to
serve Moses, never ambitious for the position God would
give him. When it had come and Moses had laid his hands
upon Joshua's shoulders and the burden of the people
with it, Caleb had seen the fear in his eyes and wondered
at God's choice. But God had been faithful. God had
molded Joshua into the leader He had intended him to be.
And God had brought them into the land He had promised
them.

It struck Caleb's heart how much he would miss this
man so many years younger than he. They had stood

together over the past forty-five years. Now, they must separate and take possession of the land God had given each of them. They must wipe Canaan clean, build homes, establish their sons. They could no longer sit together and talk or walk through the camps after evening sacrifices. Time was a cruel master. Still, they would see one another when the tribes came together for Passover at the place the Lord would establish. Surely their friendship would stand despite the distance.

O Lord, watch over and protect Joshua. Keep him strong of heart, mind, soul, and body.

Israel's captain had aged in the past five years. How much, troubled Caleb. But he could not turn away from what the Lord had called him to do: Take the hill country.

"Now, as you can see, the Lord has kept me alive and well as He promised for all these forty-five years since Moses made this promise—even while Israel wandered in the wilderness. Today I am eighty-five years old. I am as strong now as I was when Moses sent me on that journey, and I can still travel and fight as well as I could then. So I'm asking you to give me the hill country that the Lord promised me. You will remember that as scouts we found the Anakites living there in great, walled cities. But if the Lord is with me, I will drive them out of the land, just as the Lord said."

Moisture filled Joshua's eyes. They both had known this day would come. It had to come. Joshua nodded solemnly. "Kiriath-arba is yours, Caleb."

Caleb's heart quickened with joy.

Joshua grasped Caleb's arm and turned him to face the sons of Judah. He raised his voice so that all could hear. "Kiriath-arba belongs to Caleb!"

Caleb's sons rejoiced, as did the others. They didn't understand that they'd face the greatest test of their lives, but the Lord would be with them. The Lord would shine His face upon them and give them victory, if only they stood firm in their faith. For without the Lord, they wouldn't be able to stand against those who dwelt in Kiriath-arba.

Joshua clasped Caleb's hand in a hard grip. "That place has always been yours, and so it always shall be."

It had been Kiriath-arba who had set fear in the hearts of the other ten spies and made them feel like grasshoppers.

Kiriath-arba, the city inhabited by giants.

✦   ✦   ✦

"For the Lord!" Caleb raised his sword and Mesha blew the shofar. Caleb and his sons led their warriors against the Anakites, who, brash and arrogant, had mocked the Lord God of Israel and come out against Judah.

"For the Lord!" Caleb felt the strength flow into him even as the words burst from his lips. He ran with the strength of youth, feeling he could soar on eagle's wings to the top of those hills. His sword rang as it blocked an Anakite's swing. Turning, Caleb drove his shoulder hard into the man's stomach, sending him back just enough that he could drive his sword up beneath the chest armor, straight into his heart. Caleb yanked his sword free as the man crumpled. Stepping over him, he shouted the battle cry again and kept going.

The cave of Machpelah would no longer be in the possession of idol worshipers and blasphemers. He struck down two more Anakites as they came at him. The burial place of Abraham, Isaac, Jacob, and their wives would once more be held by Hebrews! He hacked into an Anakite's thigh, tumbling him, cleaving his skull as he tried to rise.

The hillsides reverberated with the cry, "For the Lord!" Caleb and his sons and the men of Judah surged up the hill, driving into the Anakites. The warriors who had once made Israel quake and refuse to enter the Promised Land melted in fear and tried to run. Caleb cried out to his sons. "Don't let them escape the judgment of the Lord!" The Anakites were pursued and cut down until the four hills on which the city stood were strewn with the dead.

Arba, the king of Kiriath-arba, was hedged in. One by one, the Anakite warriors fell.

"The king," Mesha shouted. "We have the king!"

Caleb came at a run, bursting through the lines. "*There is no king but the Lord our God!*" He brushed his son aside.

Mesha tried to block him. "What are you going to do?"

Caleb saw the fear in his son's eyes. "I'm going to kill him."

"We'll do it, Father."

"Stand aside."

Cornered, Arba glared, teeth bared. He held his mighty sword in huge hands, swinging it back and forth, spitting insults and hissing blasphemies.

Caleb strode toward him. "*Lord, give me strength!*" At his cry, his sons lowered their swords. The men of Judah held their ground and watched.

"Come to me." Arba jerked his chin up. "Come to me, you little red dog."

And Caleb came in the strength of the Lord. With one swing, he severed Arba's sword arm. With the second, he sliced along the base of Arba's chest armor so the Anakite's innards spilled out. As Arba fell to his knees, Caleb swung one last time, and sent the enemy of God into the dust.

"Cleanse the city!"

The men of Judah poured through the gates, killing every citizen, from the oldest to the youngest. They broke down the pagan altars and burned them. Household gods were put through fire, melting down the gold so the images were destroyed. The best of everything was then set aside to be delivered to Joshua for the Lord's treasury.

Caleb stood on the highest of the four hills and surveyed the land the Lord had given him. This ground on which he stood was rich in history. During his first visit, he had heard that Kiriath-arba was the oldest city in the hill country, an ancient dwelling place for Canaanite royalty, founded seven years before Tanis in Egypt. Somewhere nearby was the cave of Machpelah that served as the burial place for Abraham, who had been called out of Ur by the Lord. With him were buried his wife, Sarah, who had born the son of promise, Isaac, who married Rebekah and fathered Jacob, who had twelve sons and came to be known as Israel—one who contends with God.

Heart full, Caleb raised his hands to the Lord like a child asking to be lifted up. The strength that had pulsed through him for the battle had waned, leaving in its wake gratitude and praise.

"This place shall no longer be called Kiriath-arba." He thought of Abraham, first in faith, and knew the name it should bear. "It shall be called *beloved of God*."

Hebron. Like his grandson.

+   +   +

"You look well, my friend."

Caleb heard the tremor in Joshua's voice and could say nothing. He grasped his arms. They kissed both cheeks in greeting. Joshua did not look well. Caleb stood to one side. Joshua reached out, gesturing for him to remain close at his side as he always had.

The other elders, leaders, judges, and officials presented themselves. Joshua had summoned all Israel to Shechem, where Joseph's bones had been buried in the tract of land Jacob had bought from the sons of Hamor, the father of Shechem.

As Caleb watched, unease filled him. Perhaps he should have paid closer attention to what was happening with the other tribes. Since gaining permission to take the hill country, he had concentrated on nothing else. With Hebron now in his hands, he had made plans to put his hand to the plow again and sow crops. Surely it was time.

"The Lord has given us rest from all our enemies." Joshua spread his hands. "I am an old man now."

A faint rumbling rose from the men. Caleb frowned, studying Joshua's face. He seemed distressed, more distressed than he had seen him since the night he had fully realized God had chosen him to lead the people. Caleb turned to the others. "Be quiet. Joshua has called us here on matters of great importance."

Joshua nodded solemnly. "You have seen everything the Lord your God has done for you during my lifetime. The Lord your God has fought for you against your enemies."

As Joshua continued, speaking slowly, with great

deliberation, Caleb felt the impatience in those around him. He could almost hear their thoughts: *Why is Joshua telling us the same things he has told us countless times before?* "So be strong! Be very careful to follow all the instructions written in the Book of the Law of Moses." Joshua reminded them once again of how God had brought them into the land He had promised them, driven out the enemies before them, how it had not been their swords and bows, but God's power, that had given them the land in which they now lived, eating from vineyards and olive groves they did not plant.

"Every promise of the Lord your God has come true. Not a single one has failed!"

When Joshua looked at him, Caleb was caught by the sorrow he saw in his friend's eyes. There was a deeper purpose for this gathering, a solemn assembly. "I am old," Joshua had said. Caleb had smiled at that. For he was older still.

"But as surely as the Lord your God has given you the good things He promised, He will also bring disaster on you if you disobey Him. He will completely wipe you out from this good land He has given you. If you break the covenant of the Lord your God by worshiping and serving other gods, His anger will burn against you."

Caleb closed his eyes and bowed his head. *Have we sinned, Lord? Is that why You give this warning? Are there some among us who are already turning away?*

"So honor the Lord and serve Him wholeheartedly. Put away forever the idols your ancestors worshiped when they lived beyond the Euphrates River and in Egypt. Serve the Lord alone." Joshua's mouth twisted in derision. "But if you are unwilling to serve the Lord, then choose today whom you will serve. Would you prefer the gods your ancestors served beyond the Euphrates? Or will it be the gods of the Amorites in whose land you now live?" His mouth softened and he looked at Caleb again, eyes shining. "But as for me and my family, we will serve the Lord."

"We would never forsake the Lord and worship other gods!"

The others joined in Caleb's answer.

Hebron rose. "For the Lord our God is the one who rescued us and our ancestors from slavery in the land of Egypt."

"He performed mighty miracles before our very eyes!"

"As we traveled through the wilderness among our enemies, He preserved us."

"It was the Lord who drove out the Amorites . . ."

". . . and the other nations living here in the land."

Caleb held out his hands. "So we, too, will serve the Lord, for He alone is our God." *May the Lord hear our words and hold us to them. And may Joshua be comforted.* He had never seen Joshua so grim, so tired, so *old*.

"You are not able to serve the Lord," Joshua continued, "for He is a holy and jealous God. He will not forgive your rebellion and sins."

"No!"

"If you forsake the Lord and serve other gods, He will turn against you and destroy you, even though He has been so good to you."

"No!" Caleb cried out in anguish. "We are determined to serve the Lord!"

"You are accountable for this decision." Joshua spoke in a quiet, fierce voice. "You have chosen to serve the Lord."

"Yes!" the men cried out. "We are accountable!"

"All right, then—" Joshua clenched his hands— "destroy the idols among you, and turn your hearts to the Lord, the God of Israel."

Shock ran through Caleb. *Idols among us?* He glanced around. He saw men lower their eyes, others pale. He thought of Achan and how easy it would be for someone to hide an idol among his possessions. He turned back with a fierce anger. If he had to search every household himself, he would do so.

The people heard the message of the Lord and made a covenant there at Shechem. Joshua drew up for them the decrees and laws so that no one could say they did not know what God required of them. Everything was recorded carefully in the Book of the Law of God. Joshua took a large stone and set it up there under the oak near where the Ark of the Covenant rested. "This stone has heard everything the Lord said to us. It will be a witness to testify against you if you go back on your word to God." Joshua sent the people away, each to his own inheritance.

✦   ✦   ✦

Caleb lingered. It had been years since he had walked with Joshua. Their steps were slower now, more deliberate. Though their bodies were weakening, their friendship remained strong.

"I am filled with sorrow over the people, Caleb."

"That they will lose faith?"

"Yes. And resolve."

"We have given our vow, Joshua."

Joshua let out his breath and shook his head. He smiled sadly. "Not all men keep their vows as you do, my friend."

"The Lord will hold them to it."

"Yes, and they will suffer."

Troubled, Caleb paused. "Let an old man rest."

Joshua stood on a knoll overlooking the fertile lands around Shechem. "I feel the seeds of rebellion growing."

"Where? We will uproot them!"

"The seeds are in the heart of every man." He gripped his garment in a tight fist. "How do we change that, Caleb?"

"We have the Law, Joshua. That's why God gave it to us."

"Is it?"

"Isn't it?" Caleb wanted to shake Joshua out of his grim reverie. "The Law is as solid as the stones on which God carved it. It is the Law God has given us that will hold us together."

"Or drive us apart. All men are not as passionate about doing right as you are, Caleb. Most are eager to live in peace, even if that means compromise." Joshua spoke firmly, not as an old man whining over past days and faint worries of the future.

"What do you want me to do, Joshua? Speak openly."

"I want you to do what you have always done. Have faith in the Lord. Stand firm. Speak out when you see men weaken." He gripped Caleb's arm. "*Keep watch!* We are still at war, Caleb, though the enemy appears vanquished. We are at war and retreat is impossible."

+   +   +

Sitting in the shade of his olive tree, Caleb spotted a man running up the road. He felt a deep stirring. Closing his eyes, he bowed his head.

"Where is Caleb?" a breathless voice shouted. "*Caleb!* I must speak with Caleb!"

Sighing, Caleb rose. "I'm here."

The young man ran up the hill to him. Caleb knew him well though the years had altered him. "Ephraim, aren't you?"

"Ephraim's son, Hirah."

"I remember when your father was a boy. He followed Joshua around like a pet lamb. We——"

"Joshua is dead!"

Caleb fell silent. He couldn't take it in, didn't want to, closed his ears to it. No, not Joshua. Joshua was fifteen years younger than he. Joshua was God's anointed leader. Joshua!

"Joshua is dead." The boy dropped to his knees, hunched over, and wept.

Anguish filled Caleb and he uttered a loud cry, then tore his garments.

Oh, Lord, my friend, my friend! What will happen to Israel now? Who will lead these stubborn people? Who, Lord?

Even as the thoughts came to him, shame filled him. Who else but the Lord had led them? Who else but God Himself could be king over such a nation as Israel?

Forgive me, Lord. After all these years, I should know better than to ask such questions. Forgive me. Help me stand firm.

Caleb put his hand on the boy's head. "Rise up, Hirah. Tell me everything."

Joshua had been buried at Timnath-serah in the hill country of Ephraim north of Mount Gaash. The boy bore other grievous news. Eleazar, son of Moses' brother, Aaron, was ailing at Gibeah.

Caleb took Hirah to his home and gave him food and drink. "How have the tribes taken the news?"

"With confusion. No one knows what to do now that Joshua is dead."

Caleb scowled. "We do what the Lord has told us to do. We cleanse the land of idol worshipers and keep our covenant with Him." It had not been that many years since they had made the covenant with Joshua at Shechem. Had they forgotten everything he had said to them already?

"We are preparing to travel to Shechem for Passover. The Lord will make His will known to us. Go now, in peace."

Caleb's sons made preparations for the journey, including in the provisions plunder they had collected from the hill country villages they had conquered. Caleb wondered if they were more interested in trade than in worship. When they arrived, there was sorrow mixed with jubilation. Joshua and Eleazer were well remembered, but as the council met and men talked, Caleb realized now much work there was yet to do. Why had it been so long left undone? The tribes had received their inheritances, and still they failed to drive all the Canaanites from their land. Worse, the tribal elders were in confusion over Joshua's death.

"Who will be the first to go out and fight for us against the Canaanites?"

"How do we decide?"

What manner of men were they? When had *they* ever decided anything?

At least Phinehas, son of Eleazar, high priest of Israel, remembered. "The Lord decides!"

Lots were cast and God's answer came swiftly.

"Judah." Phinehas stood. "Judah is to go and fight. The Lord has given the land into their hands."

Once, Caleb would have been exultant. Now, he stood silent, grim with resolve while his sons and the men of Judah shouted their response. Too many in Israel lacked the faith to take and hold their land and keep it purified. Did they think Judah could do for them what God had told them they must do for themselves? Some had allowed the pagans to remain pocketed in fertile valleys or nestled in ravines. The Lord had said these idol worshipers would be like thorns in Israel's side if allowed to remain. *None* must remain.

His sons came to him. "We have made an alliance with our Simeonite brothers. If they will come up into the territory allotted to us to fight against the Canaanites, we will in turn go with them into theirs."

"Did you inquire of the Lord about this alliance?"

"They are our brothers, Father. Hasn't the Lord said from the beginning that we are to come alongside one another? Didn't you say—"

"Has every man among you forgotten what happened when we did not inquire of the Lord over the Gibeonites?"

"These are our brothers!" Mesha said.

Caleb raged. "And the Lord said *Judah* is to go! The Lord has given the land into *Judah's* hand."

They all talked at once, rationalizing and justifying their decision.

"Enough." They might as well have kicked Caleb in the stomach. Simeon! These brothers used their swords as implements of violence. Even Jacob had said not to enter into their council or be united in their assemblies, for they were cursed because of their anger and cruelty. As was

Levi. The Lord had dispersed the Levites among the tribes as priests, but what of the Simeonites? How would the Lord disperse them? And what trouble would arise if Judah aligned with them?

"When will you learn we must heed the Word of the Lord and follow Him only?"

When men made their own plans, disaster was sure to follow.

✦   ✦   ✦

Judah attacked the Canaanites at Bezek and the Lord was with them. They struck down hundreds, then thousands.

Bloodied by those he had cut down, Caleb spotted the king of Bezek with his circlet of gold. "There is Adoni-bezek." He hacked his way toward the Canaanite king, and saw the man flee the raging battle. "Don't let him escape!"

Some of the men of Judah went in pursuit. Caleb did not leave the battlefield, but roused the men of Judah and Simeon to destroy the enemies of God. Ten thousand were cut down before they could scatter in retreat. When Caleb saw Adoni-bezek, he was appalled. The man's thumbs and big toes had been chopped off. The conquered king stumbled and fell, sobbing in agony.

Caleb raged. "What have you done?"

Shelumiel, leader of the Simeonites, spoke, head high, chin jutting. "What he deserves! We have done to him what he did to the seventy kings who ate scraps under his table."

Moaning in the dust, Adoni-bezek cried out, "God has paid me back."

"Kill him," Caleb ordered. Surely there was more mercy in killing him outright than torturing and mutilating him.

"We will kill him!" Shelumiel looped a rope around the Canaanite's neck. "When we're ready." The men of Simeon laughed at the man's plight. He was led up the mountain. When he fell, they dragged him. He was given only enough water to keep him alive. When the army arrived before the city of Jerusalem, Adoni-bezek was brought up before the men and stood before the walls. Shelumiel executed him there so the Jebusites could witness his death.

Furious, Caleb ordered them to leave. "Go home. Go back to your own land!" He wanted no part of these men.

"What are you talking about? We've come to help you. You can't destroy these people without us."

"The Lord said *Judah* was to go up. Not Simeon! Would you rebel against the Lord with whom you just renewed a covenant?" Caleb looked at Adoni-bezek's body. The Lord had said to kill the Canaanites, not torture them. "Go south and fight for your land."

"You made an alliance to help us!"

"We will help you *after* we have taken Jerusalem."

The Simeonites departed, but his sons were not pleased. "How are we going to deal with the Jebusites without more men?"

Caleb was angrier with the men of Judah than with the Simeonites. "We do not *need* more men. The Lord is our strength. Trust in *Him*. Do not put your faith in men. Our victory does not depend on the number of warriors, or how many horses or chariots, *but on the power of the God who delivered us from Egypt!*"

Rallied, the men cried out to the Lord to give them help. But Caleb wondered then what the future held.

Joshua had been right in speaking to Israel that last

time in Shechem. Joshua had seen the way things were going.

And now, Caleb feared he saw as well.

+ + +

The gates were breeched, the walls scaled, the men on the battlements killed. Screams rent the air, carrying across the narrow valley in which a grove of olives grew. Every man, woman, and child who had not fled before the onslaught of Judah died within the walls. "Burn it!" Caleb commanded, and men ran with torches, setting houses, altars, and piles of wooden household gods on fire.

The army of Judah headed south and joined forces with Simeon. They fought against and defeated the Canaanites. Simeonites settled in Beersheba, Hormah, and Arad.

Judah turned north once again, fighting against the Canaanites who had come back into the hill country during their absence. Judah took the Negev and the western hills, and returned to Hebron in force, destroying the remnant of Anak who attempted to reclaim it.

"They keep coming back!"

"They're like a plague of locusts!"

Judah's army drove out the Canaanites from the hill country, killing every one of them they found. Only Caleb sent his men in pursuit of those who escaped. "The Lord was clear. If you don't finish them, they will keep coming back. Now, go after them and destroy them completely."

They obeyed until the winter months and then returned to their homes. They were tired of fighting. They wanted to celebrate their victories and tell tales of their great feats. They praised the Lord, too, but mostly they talked of what they had accomplished over the years of fighting. Areas remained unconquered; enemies hid, plotted, and spread in the recesses of the hill country.

"We will finish the work when spring comes."

When spring came, the people of Judah planted crops.

"Next year we will finish the job."

And with each year sin grew.

✦ ✦ ✦

Triumph gave way to complacency.

The Benjamites failed to hold Jerusalem. The Jebusites poured back into the city and the Benjamites could not dislodge them.

The tribe of Manasseh chose not to drive out the people of Beth-shan or Taanach or Dor or Ibleam or Megiddo nor the surrounding settlements. Instead, they made the Canaanites forced labor.

The tribe of Ephraim did not succeed in driving out the Canaanites living in Gezer.

The tribe of Zebulun allowed the Canaanites to live in Kitron and Nahalol. They did not follow the example of Manasseh, but made alliances with the people of the land and began adopting their ways.

The tribe of Asher did not drive out those living in Acco, Sidon, Ahlab, Aczib or Helbah, or in Aphek or Rehob. Asher dwelt among the people of the land.

The tribe of Naphtali left the inhabitants in Beth-shemesh and Beth-anath living in peace, and lived among them.

✦ ✦ ✦

"We can't drive them from the plains, Father."

"You must rely upon the Lord."

"We have prayed."

"We have fasted."

"We have done everything we can think to do. And we cannot drive them out."

"They have iron chariots, Father."

"At least, we hold the hill country. We hold Hebron securely. That was our own inheritance."

"And for how long will we hold it if we allow God's enemies to live?" Caleb hung his head in shame. "We have failed to do what the Lord told us to do."

"We have fought!"

"Some have died."

"The Lord is not protecting us! He is far from us!"

"Because we have sinned!" Caleb cried out in anger. "Because you lack the faith to follow the Lord."

"How have we sinned, Father? Tell us. We have worshiped the Lord just as you have."

"I have scars to show for my faith, Father! And so do countless others. I have grandchildren. I want to have time to enjoy my inheritance. Don't you?"

"We don't need the plains, Father. We have enough land here in the hill country."

Caleb could not believe what he was hearing. "We will be at war until the enemies of God are all dead like the generation who perished in the wilderness. You cannot give up. You must arm yourselves."

"We are tired of fighting!"

"We can do no more in the plains!"

"And what of Hebron?"

Mesha gazed at him, defeated. "Don't you remember, Father? Hebron no longer belongs to Judah. Joshua and the others gave it to the Levites as a city of refuge. The Kohathite clan can take care of themselves."

"Naked we come into this world, Mesha. Naked we go out of it." Caleb had been surprised when Joshua named Hebron as a city of refuge, but Joshua had done only what the Lord had told him to. Caleb had known then that he could think upon it in either of two ways: resentment, allowing bitterness and envy to grow and spread their killing vines . . . or gratitude. He chose to be thankful that God had wanted Hebron, Caleb's city, to be counted as a city of refuge.

Unfortunately, not all his sons had been able to accept the loss, or been completely content living in the surrounding villages.

"Hebron was never ours, my sons. God gave it to us, and we have given it back to Him."

"It was to be your inheritance forever, Father."

"Some of our men died in taking that city from the Anakites. It was *our* blood that was shed for that city."

"The Lord was with us."

They all talked at once.

Mesha spoke for all. "We will rest for a while, and if they attempt to come up into the hill country, then we will fight again."

Wine flowed freely, made from grapes that came from vines they did not plant, vines the Lord had given them.

Shobab sighed. "I've yet to plow a field."

Fields the Lord had given them.

"Or plant crops," Mareshah agreed.

Caleb thought of the grain that had been harvested the first years they had come into the Promised Land. The Lord had brought them in when there was a bounty of food, theirs for the taking.

"Will you know how to plant crops?" one joked.

"I can learn."

Would they ever learn what was important?

"I have work to do on my house."

What about the work God had given them to do?

"It's time for my son Hebron to take a wife."

"I have a daughter he can marry."

The men, young and old, laughed and talked on around Caleb. He rose, knowing they would take little notice of him now. They were too busy making plans for themselves. He went outside and raised his head.

Oh, God, forgive them. They know not what they do.

CALEB hobbled toward a flat stone near an ancient olive tree where he often sat overlooking the orchard and vineyard. "Come, my sons. Come. We must make plans to secure the hill country. We cannot stop the advance."

"We can't now, Father." They raised their hoes in a gesture of solidarity. "We have work to do."

Caleb's mouth tightened. He and his sons had driven out the three Anakites—Sheshai, Ahiman, and Talmai—from Hebron, but when they advanced upon Kiriath-sepher, Caleb had been too weary to go with them and they had left the work undone. Thus, the Canaanites had trickled back in like a leak in a roof. His sons, complacent, had forgotten the warnings of the Lord.

He heard his sons' grumbling. *Doesn't he ever get tired of fighting? War, war. We've had enough of war. It's time to enjoy the land we've taken. We will hold what we have.*

Oh, they knew what he was going to say. Hadn't they heard everything a hundred times before? They wanted to plow and plant seed, to enjoy the land they had taken. So what if a few Canaanites came back. *Peace, we want peace!* But they would have none. God had warned them. They just wouldn't listen.

Leaning on his walking stick, Caleb felt defeated. The spirit within him still rose to the challenge, but his body had given out. And there was no one to rally these sons of his, no one to lead them. Ever since they had reconquered Hebron, only to find it given to the Levites as a city of refuge, they had ceased listening to him.

Mesha's resentment grew with each year he tilled the

soil. Caleb grew weary of hearing the same complaints over and over again. "We fought for five years to settle the tribes. And then, our turn came and we had to take the land by ourselves! And then what happens? The biggest and best city we have is handed over to the Levites and we get the surrounding villages!"

Patiently, Caleb would explain again. "Hebron is the best of what we have. And the Lord gave it to us. Is it not right that we give God the best? Do you think we could have taken Hebron by ourselves? God gave it to us. He is the rightful owner! You cannot offer a village as a city of refuge."

Still their whining continued. "A village would have sufficed!"

"We pay in blood and the Levites reap the benefits!"

What was wrong with these sons of his? Had they set their hearts against the Lord their God? Had they forgotten already the commandments by which they were to live?

Ultimately, they gave up Hebron, then concentrated on claiming the surrounding villages and pasturelands. They drove the Canaanites out, killing every one of them that did not flee the hill country. No more was said about Hebron, but Caleb saw how they looked toward it. Their resentment spread like mildew, seeping into the cracks and walls of the houses in which they now lived, houses they had not built, but God had given them. It seemed against their very nature to be grateful for the gifts God had given them.

As the months and years wore on, Caleb's sons turned their strength and thoughts to the orchards and vineyards, flocks and herds. They prospered, but were not content.

They didn't listen to their father as they had when they were boys. They no longer hung upon his every word, nor followed his instructions, nor strove to please him and, in doing so, please God.

Often, Caleb thought back with strange longing to those hard years of wandering in the desert. The people had learned to rely upon the Lord for everything—for food, for water, for shelter, and for protection from enemies who watched and waited. Now that they had conquered the Promised Land and settled in it, life had become easier. The Israelites had relaxed their vigil, dozed in the sunshine, forgotten that faith was more work than tilling the ground.

Like so many others in Israel, his sons were doing whatever was right in their own eyes. And Caleb grieved over it, trying each day to draw them back to what they had been when times were harder. But they did not want to come or listen. Not anymore. It was by God's grace that they continued to prosper, but they had been warned when the blessings of steadfast faith and cursings of rebellion had been read to them from Mount Gerizim and Mount Ebal. Oh, they kept the Sabbaths, but without joy. What God had given them now ruled their days and nights.

When Caleb prayed with them, he felt their impatience. *Get it done and said, Father, and let us be about our work!* He could almost hear their thoughts. *Must we listen to another rambling prayer of praise from this old man?*

Oh, they loved him. He had no doubt of that. They saw to his every need and made sure he was pampered and petted. But they thought his time was over and theirs had begun. They thought he couldn't teach them anything they didn't already know. They thought times were different now.

All true, but some things must stay the same. And it was this he tried to tell them. And it was this they refused to hear.

The slippage had already begun, like a few pebbles trickling down a hillside with a boulder now and then. The people neglected the things the Lord had told them to do. The Canaanites had not been driven from every valley in the region. A few had returned, tentative at first, with words of peace and offerings of friendship. The men of Israel were too busy enjoying the milk and honey of the land God had given them to see the danger in allowing God's enemies to return and settle in small encampments. The Canaanites vowing peace gnawed like termites at the foundations God had laid.

How could his sons have forgotten what happened at Shittim? Men were easily enticed into Baal worship. *A beautiful young woman beckons, and a foolish man follows like a lamb to the slaughter.*

God demanded that His people live holy lives and not intermingle with those who had corrupted the land. All his sons could see were the healthy vines, the orchards, the houses, the wells of water. They failed to uproot and destroy every enemy of God, and now Canaanites were springing up here and there, like poisonous weeds, and their evil ways with them.

His sons and the other men of Judah had yet to take Kiriath-sepher. The fortified city was still infested with Canaanite vermin.

Caleb's twelve sons and their many sons plowed and planted, tended and harvested, believing their efforts made the difference between prosperity and poverty. And each year, they had to work a little harder.

"It is not by your strength and power that you conquered this land, but by the Spirit of the Lord!" Caleb told them.

"Someone has to plow, Father. Someone has to plant the seed."

"But it is the Lord who waters, my sons. It is the Lord who gives the sunlight and makes things grow."

"Things grew here long before we came. Canaan was a treasure trove *before* we entered it."

Caleb felt his skin prickle with alarm. He had heard that some of his sons were going after other gods. Mesha's words confirmed it. "God made it prosper. He prepared this land for us."

"So you say."

They listened less with each passing year. And like this morning, they prayed the same prayers they prayed every day, and then went off to live life on their own terms.

"Good morning, Father."

Startled from his grim thoughts, he turned. Acsah, his only daughter, the last child of his loins, came to him and slipped her arm into his. She had Maacah's dark eyes and olive skin and his red hair. *Edom,* some called her when they thought his back was turned and he couldn't hear. Had her mother sent her to tend him?

"Do you think I need help to the rock?"

"You have that look again."

Annoyed, he shook off her support and made his way toward his destination. Every joint in his body ached. His legs felt like tree trunks sending roots into the ground. Stooped, he gritted his teeth against the grinding pain and jabbed his walking stick into the ground. One deliberate step at a time.

Acsah strolled at a leisurely pace beside him, her hands clasped behind her back. He glowered at her. "Don't hover like a mother hen!"

"You're in a fine mood this morning."

Because he had fixed his gaze upon her, he stumbled. He caught himself, but not before he had seen her quick movement. His heart thundered in fury. "What would you do? Throw yourself on the ground to cushion my fall?"

"Should I stand by and watch my father dive headfirst into the ground?"

"You have work to do. Go do it."

She looked away and blinked. "I've been to the well."

Women were always too quick to tears. He didn't soften. "There are other things to do besides water the sheep and goats."

Eyes flashing, her chin came up. "Then give *me* the sword and let *me* do it."

He gave a derisive laugh and hobbled on. Maybe if he ignored her, she would go away. He groaned as he eased himself down on the flat boulder.

Lord, I can't get my sons to sit for an hour and listen to me, but this girl digs in like a tick.

Sighing deeply, he hunched in the shade of the ancient olive tree. Acsah sat within the cool circle of shade. He peered at her, still irritated. "It's time you were married." She would scurry off at that. She usually kept her distance for a few days when he mentioned her future.

"There's no one worthy enough to marry me."

"Oh!" He laughed outright at that. "You don't think much of yourself, do you? A half-caste Canaanite whelp."

Her olive skin reddened. She turned her face away.

Caleb clenched his teeth. "It's time you covered your hair."

She looked back at him. "It's time for a lot of things, Father."

"You're not a child anymore. You're—" he frowned— "how old are you?"

She stared at him without answering.

Anger bubbled up inside him. "Don't think my arm isn't long enough to deal with you."

Acsah rose gracefully and sat near enough that he could backhand her. "Anything to make your life easier, Father."

He raised his hand. She didn't draw back. He watched the pulse throb in her throat. Anger or fear? What did it matter? Releasing his breath slowly, he lowered his hand. He ignored her. The silence lengthened, but not comfortably. He cleared his throat; the sound came like a low growl. She raised one brow. He closed his eyes. Maybe if he pretended to nap.

"What were you going to say to my brothers?"

His mouth tightened. He opened one eye. "Ask them. They could tell you word for word what I was going to say. The same things I always say; the same things they always ignore."

"If you were going to tell them about the plagues of Egypt and the wandering in the wilderness, you tell the stories better than they do."

"They are not stories! I lived through those times."

"I wish I had."

He ignored the longing in her voice. "Did your mother tell you to come out and humor me?"

"Do you think I need my mother to command me to sit with you? I love you, Abba!" She looked at him, unblinking, and then bowed her head. "If I heard your stories a thousand times, Father, it would not be enough."

He said nothing and she looked up. He saw the yearning in her dark eyes, the intensity of her interest. Why was it that this girl, daughter of his concubine, had such a passion for God when his sons had so little? Overcome by despair, he cried out bitterly, "Go away. Leave me alone." What use was a girl?

She rose slowly and walked away, shoulders slumped.

Caleb regretted his harshness, but did not call her back.

The day wore on, the same as every other. Everyone had things to occupy their time and their minds. Except Caleb. He sat and waited for time to pass, waited for the sun to cross the sky and dip red-gold, orange-purple into the west. Right now, it was overhead and beating down. He wished for a cooler place, but was too weary to get up and make his way back to the house.

Caleb watched Acsah work with the wives of her brothers and half brothers. She did not seem interested in their conversation. They talked around her. They laughed. Some leaned close and whispered, eyes upon her. Caleb tried not to think about it. He tried not to let it bother him that his daughter was treated like an outsider. Even after all these years, he remembered how he had felt.

When he dozed, he dreamed of Egypt. He stood before his father again, arguing. "This is a God of gods, a Lord of lords. Wherever He leads, I will follow." When he awakened, he felt an ache in his heart so deep he had to breathe around it.

Acsah came with bread and wine. "You haven't eaten since early this morning."

"I'm not hungry."

She left it for him anyway.

After a while, he dipped the bread into the wine. When it was softened, he chewed slowly until it was a sodden mass he could swallow.

Acsah came again, bringing his great-grandchildren with her this time. "Come, come, children. Listen to Abba tell of the plagues of Egypt and the opening of the Red Sea." She sat them around him and took a place herself on the outer edge of the gathering. Gratified, Caleb spoke of the events that had shaped his faith and molded his life. It was not a quick telling, and one by one, the children rose and went away to play, until only Acsah remained.

He gave a weary sigh. "You're the only one who cares to listen."

Her eyes filled. "I wish it were not so."

His sons were returning from the fields, their hoes across their shoulders, hands draped over them. They looked weary, discontent. He looked at Acsah, still waiting, hope in her eyes. "How is it that you alone hang upon every word about the Lord our God?"

"I don't know, Father. Where did your faith come from?"

✦   ✦   ✦

Acsah's answer remained in Caleb's grieving mind. How had he come by his faith? Why was it he could not instill faith in his sons?

He lay awake upon his cushions all night, thinking. How was it that he alone among all his family members had known there was only one God with power, that all the others were counterfeit? He had grown up with the idols of Egypt, given libations and prayers as did his mother and father and his brothers and their wives. Yet, the moment Moses had returned from Midian, Caleb had known his life would never be the same. He had witnessed the plagues and known without doubt that the God of Moses, the God of Abraham was all-powerful. All the gods of Egypt could not prevail against Him, for they were nothing more than the pathetic conjuring of men's imaginations.

Faith had come to him like a flash of sunlight, a joy in his heart. *Here is a God I can worship! Here is a God I can follow with confidence and rejoicing!*

But faith had not come to his family members in the same way—reason and necessity had drawn them. Crops beaten down by hail and burned by lightning, animals dead from disease, boils making the Egyptians moan in agony, Caleb knew it had been fear that made his family listen at last to his reasoning and follow him to the Hebrew encampment. They'd never shared his excitement or joy at being in the Presence of the cloud or pillar of fire. They'd never stood in wonder and stared at the swirling canopy of light and shadow.

They followed in dread.

They obeyed out of fear.

They gave offerings because the Law required them to do so.

Surely my faith came from You, Lord, and I can't boast in it. It was born in an instant. My eyes and ears were opened. My heart beat as though for the first time. My lungs filled with the air of thanksgiving. I wanted to be counted among Your people. I wanted to live a life that would please You.

Why not my sons? Why only Acsah, a girl, last and least among all my offspring?

He wearied himself asking the questions. Whatever the reason, Acsah believed as strongly as he did. She yearned to be close to God the way he yearned. But instead of encouraging her faith, he had assumed she was patronizing him. He had been irritated at the thought of his concubines and sons humoring him, thinking he was an old man and should have someone to watch over him.

But Acsah's faith was genuine.

Only last year, when they had gone up to Jerusalem to the solemn assembly of Atonement Day, Caleb had watched her gather olive and myrtle branches and palm branches while his sons were off celebrating with their friends.

"Where is Acsah?"

"Am I my sister's keeper?"

Maacah slapped Sheva. "Go and find her. And you, too, Tirhanah." She gestured to her sons.

"She is building a booth," Caleb said.

Maacah had looked at him, perplexed. "Did you send her?"

He could see that his concubine wondered if he had lost his mind. "No. She went of her own accord."

"But why?"

He looked at his sons. "Atonement Day is followed by the Festival of the Booths."

"We haven't lived in booths since Joshua died, Father."

"No one does that anymore."

Caleb roused. "It would be good for you to remember why we wandered in the wilderness for forty years and had to live in booths!"

Into the tense silence that followed, Maacah spoke gravely. "An unmarried girl has no business living outside her father's house." His sons went to bring her back. He remembered how Acsah had fought and then, defeated, had wept.

Now they lived in a garden of God's making, and the wilderness was forgotten. So, too, were the lessons they had learned there.

Caleb knew he must do something before it was too late.

✦ ✦ ✦

I am an old man, Lord, and I cannot fight anymore. My words no longer fire men's blood. The sin in our lives is a greater threat than our enemies! We have not completed the work You set before us. I look around me and see how complacent my sons have become, how complacent the people.

We rebuild towns, but step over the rubble in our lives. We make friends with those who despise Your Name. I don't know what to do. I'm tired, worn down by despair, worn out by age. I can barely rise from my pallet now or eat my food. Servants tend me. But my mind, Lord, my mind still races. My heart still pounds out praises to Your name!

"He's crying again."

Caleb sat with his back resting against cushions propped up to support him. Was he crying? Tears seemed to come without warning these days. His body was feeble. Did they think his mind was as well? He listened to his sons talk around him. He hadn't spoken in days, his thoughts focused on God. Perhaps his silence now would cause them to open their ears when he did decide to speak again. If he did. He would say nothing until the Lord told him what to do. For now, let them wonder. He was beyond explanations, weary of trying to convince them to pursue God's will.

I wait upon You, Lord. Until I take my last breath, I wait upon You. Tell me what I am to do about my sons.

Acsah came near. She rested her hand upon his shoulder and knelt beside him, a bowl of brown muck in her hand. He scowled as he looked at it. The few teeth he had left were worn down and caused him pain. He was reduced to eating finely chopped meat and mashed vegetables. He couldn't even tell what she was offering him.

She placed the bowl in his hands. "Please, Father, eat a little. You need it to keep up your strength."

It would do no good to tell her that he had lost his sense of smell and taste and that to eat this slop tested his will.

"What ails Father?" Hur studied him from across the room.

Moza shrugged. "He's old; that's what ails him." He called to Acsah and held his cup up so she could replenish his wine.

Haran ate a date. "He hardly eats."

"He's not leading an army anymore."

"He hasn't said a word in days."

Acsah poured wine into Caleb's cup. "Perhaps he's tired of speaking and being ignored."

Her older brother Sheber scowled. "Go about your business, girl, and leave the men to theirs."

Caleb clenched his jaw. It wasn't the first time he had heard his sons speak to their sister with such disdain. Even some of his sons' wives treated her like an outsider, a servant at best. And Acsah had more faith than all of them combined.

"Perhaps his mind is going." Sheber did not appear much distressed at the possibility.

"The people still revere him. If his mind is going, we should keep quiet about it and not shame him."

Caleb felt his sons studying him. He didn't raise his head or look at them, but ate slowly with a trembling hand.

"He's praying." Acsah again, quietly, tenderly.

"For seven days straight? No man prays that long."

"Moses was on the mountain forty days and forty nights."

Sheber waved his sister off. "*Moses.* Yes. Our father believes in God, but Father was a warrior, not a prophet."

"God chose him after Joshua—"

"Hush, girl! Go feed the goats." Shaaph gestured. "Go card wool. Get out of our hair."

Caleb heard the clatter of crockery and stomping feet.

"Maybe Acsah is right. Maybe he is praying."

"We're at peace. We're prospering. What is there to pray about now?"

Caleb lost what little appetite he had. Shaking, he leaned forward to put his bowl down.

"You'd better take that from him or he'll spill it all over himself."

Hebron took the bowl and set it aside.

"I've never seen him pray longer than a few hours at one sitting." Tirhanah squinted at his father.

"We should do something about Acsah."

"What about Acsah?"

"We should find her a husband."

"Mesha's youngest daughter is a year younger than our sister, and she's married and has a son. Acsah needs sons."

"She has four brothers. She doesn't need sons."

"Besides, she's needed here."

His sons were silent just long enough for Caleb to know they were looking at him. The heat of anger surged into Caleb's face, but he did keep his silence.

Replete from the sumptuous meal, Sheber leaned back with a belch. "She's content."

Content? How little they knew or cared about their sister.

"Just leave her be. If she wants to get married, she'll say something to Father about it and he can decide what to do about her."

It was easy to see they all assumed he would do nothing because of the convenience of her tender care. He kept his head down, pretending to doze. Let them think he was a tired old man, hardly able to chew his bread. One by one, his sons rose and went out to whatever work or pleasurable activities they had planned for themselves.

Acsah returned and knelt beside him. She tore off some bread and dipped it into the wine and held the morsel to his lips. "Just a little, Father, please. Don't give up."

He looked into her eyes. The others no longer needed him. They were moving on with their lives, moving ahead without any thought of him. But she was different. She was determined to keep him going. Why? *Oh, Lord, I'm tired. I'm sick at heart. Don't let me live long enough to see my sons all turn away from You. Let me die before that day comes.* Unable to stop the tears, he bent his head and let them come, shoulders heaving.

"God of mercy and strength . . ." Acsah spoke softly, weeping as she prayed fervently. For him. "Give Father back his strength, Lord. We need him. If he lays down his head now, what will become of our people? Who will rise up to shout Your name? Who will . . . ?"

Caleb's tears ceased as he listened to his daughter. His mind opened wide, as though a hand drew aside a curtain so that he could see clearly. Did his sons love him as she did? Did they listen to him with open mind and heart, absorbing the lessons he had to teach as though his words came from the Lord Himself? *Acsah. Sweet Acsah.* A future and a hope lay before him. This girl was more like him than all his sons combined. They caused him endless grief; she lived to please him. She alone stood straight among others who bent with the wind.

"Then give me the sword!" she had cried out to him once.

A sword.

His burden lifted and he let out his breath in a long sigh. "Acsah." Trembling, he rested his hand upon her. "God has answered us."

She raised her head, eyes red and cheeks pale from weeping. Catching her breath, she sat upon her heels, eyes brightened. "What did He say, Father?" Tiny bumps rose on her arms and she leaned toward him, eager to hear.

"I must find you a husband."

She blanched. "No."

"Yes."

Her tears came again, in a storm of anger this time. "Why?" She glared at him. "You made it up. God said no such thing!"

Caleb caught her face between his hands and held her firmly, trembling. "I didn't make it up. You are to marry. Now, tell me who it is to be. Give me the name."

Her eyes went wide. "I don't know."

He opened his heart wide and sent up a prayer like an arrow to heaven. *Who, Lord? Who is to be my daughter's husband?*

Ask her.

If she didn't know the name, she must know other things. But what? What?

"Father, don't upset yourself."

"Hush." He must look wild in his frustration. He released her with a pat on her cheek. "Let an old man think." *Lord, what do I ask? What?* And then it came to him. "What sort of man would you want?"

"I have not thought about it."

"You must have thought about it. Now, tell me."

"I see the sort of men there are, and I want none of them. Why would I want any one of them to be my husband? I would rather die than—"

"Answer the question. What would it take to make you content? to bring you joy. Think!"

She clenched her hands until her knuckles were white. "Someone who loves God above everyone and everything else. Someone who keeps the covenant. Someone who doesn't look away when God's enemies move back into the land God gave us. Someone who hears God when He speaks. A man with a warrior's heart." She glared at him through her tears. *"Someone like my father!"*

He smiled ruefully. "Someone far better than your father, I think. You want a prophet."

"Nothing less." Her eyes were as fierce as a lioness's. "If I have any real choice in the matter."

"Go and fetch me your brothers."

Her defiance withered. "No, Father, please . . ."

"Do you trust me?"

She bit her lip.

He gave a curt laugh. Why *should* she trust him? Had he ever put her interests above his sons'? His eyes had been so fixed upon them that he had neglected to think much about her. But she had gleaned the Word of the Lord. She had taken up hope and held it close, nourishing her soul upon it.

"Father, let me stay with you." Tears slipped down her cheeks. "Let me serve you." She bowed her head.

He tipped her chin. "Acsah, my child. Do you trust *God?*" He already knew the answer, but wanted to hear it from her lips.

"Yes."

"Then trust in Him and go fetch your brothers. God knows the plans He has for you, and it is for your future and *our* hope."

Resigned, she rose to obey.

Caleb lifted his hands to the heavens. *In my distress, I cried out to You, Lord. And You answered.*

A leader would rise because of his daughter. And an army would go out and be victorious.

✦   ✦   ✦

Caleb looked out over the field of faces who had come at his summons. Not all the families of Judah were represented, but that didn't matter. God would have His way. Somewhere among these men was a man God would call to arms. Perhaps he had already sensed God's leading, and been troubled and unsure why. But what lay before Caleb now was certain. The one who listened and acted upon what was said today would be the one God would use to judge Israel.

The men talked among themselves, and Caleb did not have the wind to shout anymore. His sons stood around him, his grandson Hebron giving him support. How

would they take what he had to announce? He nudged
Hebron. "Call them to order."

"Silence! Let Caleb speak."

The men fell quiet.

Caleb gestured for them to come closer and they did.

"I am an old man and can no longer lead you in battle.
Another must rise to take my place."

"What of your sons? What of Mesha? or Hur?"

Caleb held his hand out and they fell silent again.

"Even now, the Lord is preparing one to lead us. Even
now—" he looked at the faces of the men gathered close—
"one of you . . ." His eyes were not as they once were and
his vision was blurred. "I have called you here to remind
you of the work yet to be done. Canaanites still inhabit
Kiriath-sepher. God told us to take this land and drive the
inhabitants out. God's enemies are emboldened by our
lack of action. We must finish the work God gave us to do.
We did not enter into the land to make peace with God's
enemies, but to destroy them!"

Some of the men shouted in agreement, but his sons
were not among them. Perhaps the one whom God had
called here would renew the vision and quicken the spirit
to obey the Lord. *Let it be so, Lord. Let it be so!*

"Father." Hur bent close. "Is that all you wish to say?"

They were so impatient, so eager to be about their own
business. They had no time for contemplation.

"No." Caleb had so much more to say, words they had
heard so many times before. They were like their fathers
before them, slow to obey the Lord, quick to forget Him.
If he said what he had said so many times before, they
would not listen. *Lord, how do You bear us? It is a wonder*

*You didn't wipe us from the face of the earth after we tested
You so many times in the desert!*

Wrath fired his blood, but wisdom made him speak
briefly. "The Lord God of Abraham, Isaac, and Jacob gave
me the hill country. My sons have claimed their portions
and have settled their families upon it. But there is still
land to conquer, land God gave me that has not yet been
claimed. I give the Negev to my daughter Acsah as her
inheritance."

He heard the hiss of the drawn breath of his sons.

"Acsah?"

Caleb raised his voice. "The daughters of Zelophehad
stood before Moses and Eleazar and the leaders and the
entire congregation, and were given land to possess among
their father's brothers. I have many sons. Mesha, my firstborn, has received his double portion. A son has been
raised up for Ardon, killed in battle, and he has received
his portion. The others have their portions of the land we
have taken. But the Lord God gave me the Negev as well,
and Kiriath-sepher is once again in the possession of the
Anakites. The portion not yet conquered shall belong to
my daughter, whose faith is like a fire within her. Mighty
men shall come from her!"

He jammed his walking stick into the ground and
stepped forward. "Hear me, sons of Judah. I will give my
daughter Acsah in marriage to the man who attacks and
captures Kiriath-sepher!"

✦   ✦   ✦

Caleb heard running feet and struggled to raise himself on
his pallet. Acsah hastened to him and helped him sit up,
pressing cushions behind him.

He heard a man speaking breathlessly outside. "Come!" Caleb called. "Enter in!" He put his hand over Acsah's. She was trembling and pale, her eyes huge and dark.

Hur's son Salma came in, face streaked with dust and sweat. He went to his knees and bowed low. "Kiriath-sepher is in our hands. The Anakites are no more!"

Caleb sat up straight, shaking violently from the effort. "Who led?"

"Othniel!" The boy raised his head, eyes shining. "Othniel, son of Kenaz!" He stood and raised his hand. "He broke through their gates and destroyed the enemy. His hand was heavy against them. They fell to his right and to his left. He did not rest until they were no more!" Salma described the battle in detail, his face alight with excitement and triumph. "The Lord our God gave Kiriath-sepher into our hands!"

Caleb saw that Othniel had done more than take Kiraith-sepher. He had fired up the sons of Judah. And if this young man was any indication, perhaps he had even turned Caleb's sons' hearts back toward the Lord. His throat tightened with tears of thanksgiving. Oh, that Kenaz, Caleb's youngest brother, the first among his family members who had followed him to the camp of the Israelites, could see this day. Caleb gave thanks to God that it was one among his own flesh and blood who now stood before Israel and called them back to faith. "The Lord is our strength and deliverer!"

"Blessed be the name of the Lord." Acsah bowed her head.

"Acsah." Caleb placed his hand upon her. She raised her head and looked into his eyes. Hers softened with love and pooled with tears. She took his hand and kissed it fervently. Then she rose and left him.

Caleb gestured to Salma. "I wish to be outside." He wanted to see the comings and goings of those he loved. Salma helped him up. He gave him support as Caleb hobbled outside and sat beneath the shade of the olive tree. He rested his back against the ancient trunk. "My sons?"

"All are well."

"Thanks be to God." Caleb gave the boy his blessing and sent him away. Then Caleb waited and looked out over the hill country. Othniel would come, and would bring Mesha and the rest of his sons and grandsons with him.

A flurry of excited activity gained Caleb's attention. Startled, he saw Acsah come out of his house garbed in wedding finery. Covered as she was with veils, he could not see her face. She spoke to a servant and stood in the sunshine waiting. A donkey was brought to her. She turned to him again and bowed her head in deep respect. She remained that way for a long moment and then straightened. Then she mounted the donkey and rode away.

All had misjudged this girl, including him. She didn't wait for her husband to come to her, but rode out to meet him. She tapped the side of the donkey with a stick so the animal trotted more quickly. He smiled. At least she wasn't dragging her feet and going out with misgivings and hesitance. No, she went out eagerly to meet the man God had chosen for her.

As the distance widened between them and Acsah became smaller, Caleb felt sorrow mingle with joy. Until this moment when he watched her ride away, he had not realized how much comfort he received from his daughter's presence.

Never had he felt so alone.

✦   ✦   ✦

Days passed slowly and then word came that his sons were returning, Othniel at their head and Acsah with them.

"Acsah!" Too weak now to rise from his pallet, Caleb told the servants to take him outside. They lifted him and carried him out and made him comfortable so that he could see the procession coming up to his village. Acsah rode beside her husband, not behind him.

Othniel came to him first and greeted him with the respect due a father. And then, blushing, he asked for a field already producing grain. Taken aback, Caleb thought about it for a moment. It would take time to tame the Negev. Caleb granted his request. Next Caleb's sons came, kissing him and talking excitedly of the battle. They then dispersed to their families.

Othniel went to Acsah and spoke to her. She smiled and put her hands upon her husband's shoulders, alighting gracefully from her donkey. She said something to Othniel. He shook his head. She spoke again and came toward Caleb. She was no longer veiled, but her hair was covered. She had become a woman in the past few days, for there was an air about her that was different. She knelt close to Caleb, her hands loosely clasped in her lap.

"Thank you for granting my husband a field, Father."

Caleb raised his brows. "Did you suggest he ask for it?"

She blushed as her husband had. "We must have grain to sustain ourselves until all the enemies of God are driven from the Negev."

"Provisions." He lowered his head and peered at her. "What is it? What can I do for you?"

She took a deep breath. "Give me a further blessing.

You have been kind enough to give me land in the Negev; please give me springs as well."

Caleb smiled. She was shrewd as well as courageous. He'd only thought of the land, not the provisions needed to take it. "The upper and lower springs are yours."

It was time to celebrate, time to feast and give thanks. He watched his sons dance in the firelight and listened to their songs of praise. His daughter danced with the women, her face alight as she twirled and raised her hands.

Caleb dozed for a while, replete and deeply satisfied. When he awakened, the celebration was still going on, the stars twinkling in the canopy of the night sky. He saw Acsah and Othniel standing in the rim of firelight, off by themselves, talking. Othniel lifted his hand and touched her. It was a gesture of tenderness. When Acsah stepped closer and reached up to her husband, Caleb closed his eyes.

Othniel and Acsah came to him before they headed south. He knew it was the last time he would see his daughter, for he was an old man with death fast approaching. When she knelt before him, he held her face between his hands and looked long into her eyes. "Do not weep so."

"How can I not weep?" She fell into his arms and buried her face in his shoulder.

"I have lived a long life and been a witness to God's signs and wonders. Could any man ask for a greater blessing? And now, I hold hope for the future. I hold that hope in you." His arms tightened around her briefly. "Your husband awaits." As she drew back, he cupped her face and kissed her cheeks and forehead. "May the Lord bless you with many God-fearing sons."

She smiled through her tears. "And daughters."

"May all your children be like you."

Othniel helped her to her feet and left his hand lightly upon her, a possessive gesture that pleased Caleb. He knew he had gained something precious, something to be protected and cherished. A wise man who saw what he himself had missed for far too long.

Caleb held his hands out as though to embrace them both. "May righteousness go before you, and the glory of the Lord be your rear guard."

He couldn't watch them ride away. They were followed by Othniel's relatives and some of his own grandsons, eager now to wage war and drive God's enemies from the land.

May they succeed this time, Lord. May they not pause to rest until every last enemy is vanquished!

But Caleb knew men were weak. They were like sheep in desperate need of a shepherd. As long as they had one, they followed. *May all their shepherds be upright, honest men of integrity who will hold fast to Your laws and statutes, Lord.*

We will rise up in faith and then fall into sin again, won't we, Lord? Is that our destiny?

The servants came out to lift his pallet. "No. Leave me here a little longer." He gestured impatiently when they hovered. "Go!" As they turned to obey, he called them back. "Bring me my sword." Troubled, they hesitated. "My sword!"

A young man ran to do Caleb's bidding and brought the weapon back. He bent down reverently, presenting the hilt to Caleb.

Caleb held his sword once more. He remembered a time when he would go into battle with this sword, swinging it to the right and left for hours without tiring. Now, he barely had the strength to lift it. Arm trembling, he used all his will not to drop it. "Go now."

How is it, Lord, that within this aging husk of a body my heart still beats for battle? I remember the day I pounded my plowshare into this sword. I thought a day would come when I would heat it in the fire and place it upon the anvil and make another plowshare. But it was not to be. Even now, I know the battle is far from over.

We cried for a deliverer and You sent us Moses. When Pharaoh refused to let Your people go, You sent plagues upon Egypt. You opened the sea for our escape and closed it over the army of Your enemies. You sheltered us with a cloud by day and protected us as a pillar of fire by night. You fed us manna from heaven and water from a rock. You satisfied my thirsty soul and filled my hungry heart with what is good and lasting.

Caleb dozed in the afternoon sun, his strength seeping, his breath slowing. He saw a temple rise, shining white with gold, glorious. A strong wind came up and blew across the land, and the temple crumbled. People wailed as they were led away in chains. And then another procession back up the mountain and another temple rose, less grand, then walls around it and a man upon the battlements calling out to the workers. "Do not be afraid. Do not grow weary. Finish the work God has given you!" But again, destruction came, again a temple rose, grander still. And light came so bright that Caleb felt pain, such pain, he moaned and clutched at his heart. *Oh, God, oh, God, will You have to do that? You are perfect! You are holy!* And then the heavens darkened, but brightened again, light spreading slowly across the land like a new dawn.

Once again destruction came.

Caleb's soul cried out in agony. His heart broke. *Oh, Lord, will it ever be so? Oh, Lord, Lord!*

The heavens opened and there came One riding a white horse, riding from the swirling clouds, riding swiftly with a sword in His hand, and upon Him emblazoned *Faithful and True, the Word of God.* Armies came with Him, clothed in fine linen, white and clean, following Him. Caleb heard the blast of the shofar. Eager to obey the call to battle, he grasped the hilt of his sword, half rising from his pallet. "Lord! *Yes!*"

King of kings, Lord of Lords!

A myriad singing. "Holy! Holy! Holy!"

Caleb drew in his breath at the blaze of colors: reds, yellows, blues, purples. Light streaming, water rushing, life pulsing.

Wait, and you will see.

Releasing his breath in a long, slow sigh, Caleb let his sword drop to his side. He closed his eyes. For now, he could rest.

For he knew one day he would awaken and rise again in strength.

DEAR READER,

We hope you enjoyed this fictional account of the life of Caleb, tribal leader, half-breed, scout, and beloved of God. This powerful story of faith and obedience by Francine Rivers is meant to whet your appetite. Francine's first and foremost desire is to take you back to God's Word to decide for yourself the truth about Caleb—his persistence, his promises, and his source of peace.

The following Bible study is designed to guide you through Scripture to *seek* the truth about Caleb and to *find* applications for your own life.

Caleb's walk with God enabled him to trust God even when circumstances screamed "not fair!" His loyalty required obedience at all costs. His trust in God's promises provided calmness in the midst of turmoil. Caleb's faith remained steadfast and growing throughout his life. It energized him in old age to aspire to all that God had promised.

May God bless you as you seek Him for the answers to your life's turmoils and inequities. And may He find you faithful and resolute in your journey with Him.

Peggy Lynch

SEEK GOD'S WORD FOR TRUTH
Read the following passage:

The Lord now said to Moses, "Send men to explore the land of Canaan, the land I am giving to Israel. Send one leader from each of the twelve ancestral tribes." So Moses did as the Lord commanded him. He sent out twelve men, all tribal leaders of Israel, from their camp in the wilderness of Paran. These were the tribes and the names of the leaders:

Tribe	Leader
Reuben	Shammua son of Zaccur
Simeon	Shaphat son of Hori
Judah	Caleb son of Jephunneh
Issachar	Igal son of Joseph
Ephraim	Hoshea son of Nun
Benjamin	Palti son of Raphu
Zebulun	Gaddiel son of Sodi
Manasseh son of Joseph	Gaddi son of Susi
Dan	Ammiel son of Gemalli
Asher	Sethur son of Michael
Naphtali	Nahbi son of Vophsi
Gad	Geuel son of Maki

These are the names of the men Moses sent to explore the land. By this time Moses had changed Hoshea's name to Joshua.   NUMBERS 13:1-16

The very first mention of Caleb in Scripture is found in this passage. Who was Caleb? What position did he hold?

What would it take to acquire and maintain this position?

Read the following passage:

Moses gave the men these instructions as he sent them out to explore the land: "Go northward through the Negev into the hill country. See what the land is like and find out whether the people living there are strong or weak, few or many. What kind of land do they live in? Is it good or bad? Do their towns have walls or are they unprotected? How is the soil? Is it fertile or poor? Are there many trees? Enter the land boldly, and bring back samples of the crops you see." (It happened to be the season for harvesting the first ripe grapes.)

So they went up and explored the land from the wilderness of Zin as far as Rehob, near Lebo-hamath. Going northward, they passed first through the Negev and arrived at Hebron, where Ahiman, Sheshai, and Talmai—all descendants of Anak—lived. (The ancient town of Hebron was founded seven years before the Egyptian city of Zoan.) When they came to what is now known as the valley of Eshcol, they cut down a cluster of grapes so large that it took two of them to carry it on a pole between them! They also took samples of the pomegranates and figs. At that time the Israelites renamed the valley Eshcol—"cluster"—because of the cluster of grapes they had cut there.

After exploring the land for forty days, the men returned to Moses, Aaron, and the people of Israel at Kadesh in the wilderness of Paran. They reported to the whole community what they had seen and showed them the fruit they had taken from the land. This was their report to Moses: "We arrived in the land you sent us to see, and it is indeed a magnificent country—a land flowing with milk and honey. Here is some of its fruit as proof. But the people living there are powerful, and their cities and towns are fortified and very large. We also saw the descendants of Anak who are living there! The Amalekites live in the Negev, and the Hittites, Jebusites, and Amorites live in the hill country. The Canaanites live along the coast of the Mediterranean Sea and along the Jordan Valley."

But Caleb tried to encourage the people as they stood before Moses. "Let's go at once to take the land," he said. "We can certainly conquer it!"

But the other men who had explored the land with him answered, "We can't go up against them! They are stronger than we are!" So they spread discouraging reports about the land among the Israelites: "The land we explored will swallow up any who go to live there. All the people we saw were huge. We even saw giants there, the descendants of Anak. We felt like grasshoppers next to them, and that's what we looked like to them!"   NUMBERS 13:17-33

What instructions were given to the twelve men? How much time did they have to complete their mission?

What did the men find? What evidence did they bring back with them?

What was the nature of the scouts' report? What was their attitude like?

What was Caleb's report? How was his attitude different?

FIND GOD'S WAYS FOR YOU
Describe a time you followed the crowd. What was the result? What did you learn?

Describe a time you stood alone. What was the outcome? How did you feel?

O Lord, you are my refuge; never let me be disgraced. Rescue me! Save me from my enemies, for you are just. Turn your ear to listen and set me free. Be to me a protecting rock of safety, where I am always welcome.   PSALM 71:1-3

What are some reasons why we need not fear standing alone?

STOP AND PONDER

For I can do everything with the help of Christ who gives me the strength I need.   PHILIPPIANS 4:13

SEEK GOD'S WORD FOR TRUTH
Read the following passage:

Then all the people began weeping aloud, and they cried all
night. Their voices rose in a great chorus of complaint against
Moses and Aaron. "We wish we had died in Egypt, or even
here in the wilderness!" they wailed. "Why is the Lord taking
us to this country only to have us die in battle? Our wives and
little ones will be carried off as slaves! Let's get out of here and
return to Egypt!" Then they plotted among themselves, "Let's
choose a leader and go back to Egypt!"

Then Moses and Aaron fell face down on the ground before
the people of Israel. Two of the men who had explored the
land, Joshua son of Nun and Caleb son of Jephunneh, tore
their clothing. They said to the community of Israel, "The
land we explored is a wonderful land! And if the Lord is
pleased with us, he will bring us safely into that land and
give it to us. It is a rich land flowing with milk and honey,
and he will give it to us! Do not rebel against the Lord, and
don't be afraid of the people of the land. They are only helpless prey to us! They have no protection, but the Lord is with
us! Don't be afraid of them!"

But the whole community began to talk about stoning
Joshua and Caleb. Then the glorious presence of the Lord
appeared to all the Israelites from above the Tabernacle. And
the Lord said to Moses, "How long will these people reject
me? Will they never believe me, even after all the miraculous
signs I have done among them? I will disown them and
destroy them with a plague. Then I will make you into a
nation far greater and mightier than they are!"

"But what will the Egyptians think when they hear about
it?" Moses pleaded with the Lord. "They know full well the
power you displayed in rescuing these people from Egypt.
They will tell this to the inhabitants of this land, who are

well aware that you are with this people. They know, Lord,
that you have appeared in full view of your people in the
pillar of cloud that hovers over them. They know that you
go before them in the pillar of cloud by day and the pillar
of fire by night. Now if you slaughter all these people, the
nations that have heard of your fame will say, 'The Lord was
not able to bring them into the land he swore to give them,
so he killed them in the wilderness.'"   NUMBERS 14:1-16

Describe the camp atmosphere after the scouting reports. What
plans did the people propose?

When Moses and Aaron fell facedown on the ground, what words
of comfort did Caleb and Joshua offer? What warning did they
give?

What specifically demonstrated the faith of Caleb and Joshua?

How did the people respond to the warnings?

Describe God's response to the people's behavior.

FIND GOD'S WAYS FOR YOU
Discuss a time when you were a mediator. Why is this event memorable?

What advice did you offer? What was the outcome?

> People who despise advice will find themselves in trouble; those who respect it will succeed. The advice of the wise is like a life-giving fountain; those who accept it avoid the snares of death. PROVERBS 13:13-14

Apply these verses to Caleb and the Israelites. Apply them to yourself.

STOP AND PONDER

Whoever walks with the wise will become wise; whoever walks with fools will suffer harm.   PROVERBS 13:20

SEEK GOD'S WORD FOR TRUTH
Read the following passage:

[Moses said,] "Please, Lord, prove that your power is as great as you have claimed it to be. For you said, 'The Lord is slow to anger and rich in unfailing love, forgiving every kind of sin and rebellion. Even so he does not leave sin unpunished, but he punishes the children for the sins of their parents to the third and fourth generations.' Please pardon the sins of this people because of your magnificent, unfailing love, just as you have forgiven them ever since they left Egypt."

Then the Lord said, "I will pardon them as you have requested. But as surely as I live, and as surely as the earth is filled with the Lord's glory, not one of these people will ever enter that land. They have seen my glorious presence and the miraculous signs I performed both in Egypt and in the wilderness, but again and again they tested me by refusing to listen. They will never even see the land I swore to give their ancestors. None of those who have treated me with contempt will enter it. But my servant Caleb is different from the others. He has remained loyal to me, and I will bring him into the land he explored. His descendants will receive their full share of that land. Now turn around and don't go on toward the land where the Amalekites and Canaanites live. Tomorrow you must set out for the wilderness in the direction of the Red Sea. "   NUMBERS 14:17-25

List all you learn about God's character from Moses' prayer.

What does this prayer tell you about Moses?

What is God's plan for the people now? Why?

What new instruction was given to the people?

How does God describe Caleb?

What is God's plan for Caleb and his family?

SEEK GOD'S WAYS FOR YOU
To whom do you turn in crises? Why?

What does this reveal about you?

How do you think God would describe you?

STOP AND PONDER

> Dear brothers and sisters, whenever trouble comes your way,
> let it be an opportunity for joy. For when your faith is tested,
> your endurance has a chance to grow. So let it grow, for
> when your endurance is fully developed, you will be strong
> in character and ready for anything.   JAMES 1:2-4

SEEK GOD'S WORD FOR TRUTH
Read the following passage:

> Then the Lord said to Moses and Aaron, "How long will this wicked nation complain about me? I have heard everything the Israelites have been saying. Now tell them this: 'As surely as I live, I will do to you the very things I heard you say. I, the Lord, have spoken! You will all die here in this wilderness! Because you complained against me, none of you who are twenty years old or older and were counted in the census will enter the land I swore to give you. The only exceptions will be Caleb son of Jephunneh and Joshua son of Nun.
>
> " 'You said your children would be taken captive. Well, I will bring them safely into the land, and they will enjoy what you have despised. But as for you, your dead bodies will fall in this wilderness. And your children will be like shepherds, wandering in the wilderness forty years. In this way, they will pay for your faithlessness, until the last of you lies dead in the wilderness.
>
> " 'Because the men who explored the land were there for forty days, you must wander in the wilderness for forty years—a year for each day, suffering the consequences of your sins. You will discover what it is like to have me for an enemy.' I, the Lord, have spoken! I will do these things to every member of the community who has conspired against me. They will all die here in this wilderness!"
>
> Then the ten scouts who had incited the rebellion against the Lord by spreading discouraging reports about the land were struck dead with a plague before the Lord. Of the twelve who had explored the land, only Joshua and Caleb remained alive.
>
> When Moses reported the Lord's words to the Israelites, there was much sorrow among the people. So they got up early the next morning and set out for the hill country of

Canaan. "Let's go," they said. "We realize that we have sinned, but now we are ready to enter the land the Lord has promised us."

But Moses said, "Why are you now disobeying the Lord's orders to return to the wilderness? It won't work. Do not go into the land now. You will only be crushed by your enemies because the Lord is not with you. When you face the Amalekites and Canaanites in battle, you will be slaughtered. The Lord will abandon you because you have abandoned the Lord."

But the people pushed ahead toward the hill country of Canaan, despite the fact that neither Moses nor the Ark of the Lord's covenant left the camp.   NUMBERS 14:26-44

Discuss the camp from God's perspective.

What do you learn about the people at this point?

What consequences befell the twelve scouts? What exceptions were made?

What consequences were exacted on the entire camp without exceptions?

What warnings did Moses give to the people? How did they react?

What did this reveal about the Israelites' relationship with Moses and with God?

FIND GOD'S WAYS FOR YOU

Discuss a time you had to live with the consequences of what someone else did. How did you feel?

Share a time when you were spared consequences you deserved. How did that feel?

No discipline is enjoyable while it is happening—it is pain-ful! But afterward there will be a quiet harvest of right living for those who are trained in this way.   HEBREWS 12:11

What do we learn about discipline from this verse? What are the conditions for "harvest"?

STOP AND PONDER

Dear brothers and sisters, I plead with you to give your bod-ies to God. Let them be a living and holy sacrifice—the kind he will accept. When you think of what he has done for you, is this too much to ask? Don't copy the behavior and customs of this world, but let God transform you into a new person by changing the way you think. Then you will know what God wants you to do, and you will know how good and pleasing and perfect his will really is.

ROMANS 12:1-2

SEEK GOD'S WORD FOR TRUTH
Read the following passage:

> After the death of Moses the Lord's servant, the Lord spoke
> to Joshua son of Nun, Moses' assistant. He said, "Now that my
> servant Moses is dead, you must lead my people across the Jor-
> dan River into the land I am giving them. I promise you what
> I promised Moses: 'Everywhere you go, you will be on land
> I have given you—from the Negev Desert in the south to the
> Lebanon mountains in the north, from the Euphrates River on
> the east to the Mediterranean Sea on the west, and all the land
> of the Hittites.' No one will be able to stand their ground
> against you as long as you live. For I will be with you as I was
> with Moses. I will not fail you or abandon you.   JOSHUA 1:1-5

Who succeeded Moses as camp leader? What is significant of this?

Read the following passage:

> When Joshua was an old man, the Lord said to him, "You are
> growing old, and much land remains to be conquered. The
> people still need to occupy the land of the Philistines and the
> Geshurites—territory that belongs to the Canaanites.
> "I will drive these people out of the land for the Israelites.
> So be sure to give this land to Israel as a special possession,
> just as I have commanded you. Include all this territory as
> Israel's inheritance when you divide the land among the nine
> tribes and the half-tribe of Manasseh."

A delegation from the tribe of Judah, led by Caleb son of Jephunneh the Kenizzite, came to Joshua at Gilgal. Caleb said to Joshua, "Remember what the Lord said to Moses, the man of God, about you and me when we were at Kadesh-barnea. I was forty years old when Moses, the servant of the Lord, sent me from Kadesh-barnea to explore the land of Canaan. I returned and gave from my heart a good report, but my brothers who went with me frightened the people and discouraged them from entering the Promised Land. For my part, I followed the Lord my God completely. So that day Moses promised me, 'The land of Canaan on which you were just walking will be your special possession and that of your descendants forever, because you wholeheartedly followed the Lord my God.'

"Now, as you can see, the Lord has kept me alive and well as he promised for all these forty-five years since Moses made this promise—even while Israel wandered in the wilderness. Today I am eighty-five years old. I am as strong now as I was when Moses sent me on that journey, and I can still travel and fight as well as I could then. So I'm asking you to give me the hill country that the Lord promised me. You will remember that as scouts we found the Anakites living there in great, walled cities. But if the Lord is with me, I will drive them out of the land, just as the Lord said."

So Joshua blessed Caleb son of Jephunneh and gave Hebron to him as an inheritance. Hebron still belongs to the descendants of Caleb son of Jephunneh the Kenizzite because he wholeheartedly followed the Lord, the God of Israel. (Previously Hebron had been called Kiriath-arba. It had been named after Arba, a great hero of the Anakites.)

And the land had rest from war.   JOSHUA 13:1-3, 6-7; 14:6-15

How did Caleb approach Joshua about Moses' promise?

As Caleb laid out his case, what did he offer as past, present, and future evidence?

How did Joshua respond to Caleb's request?

What proclamation about God does Caleb make that is like Moses?

What reason is given for Caleb's inheritance? What does this tell you about his relationship with God?

FIND GOD'S WAYS FOR YOU

How do you approach people when reminding them of a promise? How has it worked out?

How have you responded when someone has approached you about a promise you made?

If you need wisdom—if you want to know what God wants you to do—ask him, and he will gladly tell you. He will not resent your asking.   JAMES 1:5

What advice does this verse offer?

STOP AND PONDER

God blesses the people who patiently endure testing. Afterward they will receive the crown of life that God has promised to those who love him.   JAMES 1:12

SEEK GOD'S WORD FOR TRUTH
Read the following passage:

> After Joshua died, the Israelites asked the Lord, "Which tribe should attack the Canaanites first?"
>
> The Lord answered, "Judah, for I have given them victory over the land."
>
> Judah marched against the Canaanites in Hebron (formerly called Kiriath-arba), defeating the forces of Sheshai, Ahiman, and Talmai. From there they marched against the people living in the town of Debir (formerly called Kiriath-sepher).
>
> Then Caleb said, "I will give my daughter Acsah in marriage to the one who attacks and captures Kiriath-sepher." Othniel, the son of Caleb's younger brother Kenaz, was the one who conquered it, so Acsah became Othniel's wife.
>
> When Acsah married Othniel, she urged him to ask her father for an additional field. As she got down off her donkey, Caleb asked her, "What is it? What can I do for you?"
>
> She said, "Give me a further blessing. You have been kind enough to give me land in the Negev; please give me springs as well." So Caleb gave her the upper and lower springs.
>
> JUDGES 1:1-2, 10-15

After Joshua died, the tribe of Judah was selected to lead the taking of the Caananite land. Who was the tribal leader? What significance do you find in this?

What incentive does Caleb offer the man who will secure the area of Kiriath-sepher?

Who accomplishes this feat? How does Caleb keep his word?

How would you describe Caleb's relationship with his daughter? What similarities do you see between the two of them?

Read the following passage:

> After that generation died, another generation grew up who did not acknowledge the Lord or remember the mighty things he had done for Israel. Then the Israelites did what was evil in the Lord's sight and worshiped the images of Baal. They abandoned the Lord, the God of their ancestors, who had brought them out of Egypt. They chased after other gods, worshiping the gods of the people around them. And they angered the Lord. They abandoned the Lord to serve Baal and the images of Ashtoreth.
>
> Then the Lord raised up judges to rescue the Israelites from their enemies.
>
> The Israelites did what was evil in the Lord's sight. They

forgot about the Lord their God, and they worshiped the
images of Baal and the Asherah poles. Then the Lord burned
with anger against Israel, and he handed them over to King
Cushan-rishathaim of Aram-naharaim. And the Israelites were
subject to Cushan-rishathaim for eight years.

But when Israel cried out to the Lord for help, the Lord
raised up a man to rescue them. His name was Othniel, the
son of Caleb's younger brother, Kenaz. The Spirit of the Lord
came upon him, and he became Israel's judge. He went to war
against King Cushan-rishathaim of Aram, and the Lord gave
Othniel victory over him. So there was peace in the land for
forty years. Then Othniel son of Kenaz died.

JUDGES 2:10-13, 16; 3:7-11

What happened after Joshua and Caleb's generation died? What
did God do to help the people?

Who was Israel's first judge and how did he become a judge?
What, if any, similarities to Caleb do you find in him?

FIND GOD'S WAYS FOR YOU
What is Caleb's most outstanding trait? Why do you think so?

In what ways do you identify with Caleb? What have you learned about yourself from this study?

What have you learned about God from Caleb's experiences?

STOP AND PONDER

> Dear brothers and sisters, let me say one more thing as I close this letter. Fix your thoughts on what is true and honorable and right. Think about things that are pure and lovely and admirable. Think about things that are excellent and worthy of praise. Keep putting into practice all you learned from me and heard from me and saw me doing, and the God of peace will be with you.   PHILIPPIANS 4:8-9

Caleb often despaired because of his inability to follow the law that God had given to His people. Hundreds of years later, the apostle Paul would speak of this same struggle:

> "I love God's law with all my heart. But there is another law at work within me that is at war with my mind. This law wins the fight and makes me a slave to the sin that is still within me. Oh, what a miserable person I am! Who will free me from this life that is dominated by sin? Thank God! The answer is in Jesus Christ our Lord." ROMANS 7:22-25

Interestingly, there are parallels between the lives of Caleb and Jesus:

CALEB
- Questionable birthright
- Of the tribe of Judah
- Endured unfair consequences as a result of others' actions
- War hero of Judah
- Committed to completing his mission—clearing the land of enemiesso God's people might live in it
- Commander of Israel's army, fighting for God and for his family
- Believed and relied on the Word of God
- A prayer warrior armed for battle

JESUS
- Questionable birthright
- Of the tribe of Judah (Rev. 5:5)
- Endured unfair execution as a result of our actions (2 Cor. 5:21)

- Lion of Judah (Rev. 5:5)
- Committed to completing His mission—clearing our lives of sin so God Himself might live in us (John 6:56)
- Commander of the armies of heaven, fighting our spiritual battles (Rev. 19:11-16)
- Is the Word of God (John 1:1)
- Is our armor and intercedes for us (Eph. 6:10-18; Heb. 7:24-25)

The same armor that covered Caleb spiritually is available to us today. In his letter to the Christians at Ephesus, the apostle Paul wrote:

A final word: Be strong with the Lord's mighty power. Put on all of God's armor so that you will be able to stand firm against all strategies and tricks of the Devil. For we are not fighting against people made of flesh and blood, but against the evil rulers and authorities of the unseen world, against those mighty powers of darkness who rule this world, and against wicked spirits in the heavenly realms. Use every piece of God's armor to resist the enemy in the time of evil, so that after the battle you will still be standing firm. Stand your ground, putting on the sturdy belt of truth and the body armor of God's righteousness. For shoes, put on the peace that comes from the Good News, so that you will be fully prepared. In every battle you will need faith as your shield to stop the fiery arrows aimed at you by Satan. Put on salvation as your helmet, and take the sword of the Spirit, which is the word of God. Pray at all times and on every occasion in the power of the Holy Spirit. Stay alert and be persistent in your prayers for all Christians everywhere.

EPHESIANS 6:10-18

FRANCINE RIVERS has been writing for more than twenty years. From 1976 to 1985 she had a successful writing career in the general market and won numerous awards. After becoming a born-again Christian in 1986, Francine wrote *Redeeming Love* as her statement of faith.

Since then, Francine has published numerous books in the CBA market and has continued to win both industry acclaim and reader loyalty. Her novel *The Last Sin Eater* won the ECPA Gold Medallion, and three of her books have won the prestigious Romance Writers of America Rita Award.

Francine uses her writing to draw closer to the Lord, that through her work she might worship and praise Jesus for all He has done and is doing in her life.

BOOKS BY BELOVED AUTHOR
FRANCINE RIVERS

OVER 2.5 MILLION SOLD!

A Lineage of Grace series

Unveiled ....ISBN 0-8423-1947-6
Unashamed..ISBN 0-8423-3596-X
Unshaken..ISBN 0-8423-3597-8
Unspoken..ISBN 0-8423-3598-6
Unafraid...ISBN 0-8423-3599-4

And the Shofar Blew

Hardcover...ISBN 0-8423-6582-6
Softcover...ISBN 0-8423-6583-4
Audio—CD ....ISBN 0-8423-6585-0

Sons of Encouragement series

The Priest ....ISBN 0-8423-8265-8
The Warrior...ISBN 0-8423-8266-6
The Prince (coming early 2006)........................ISBN 0-8423-8267-4
The Prophet (Fall 2006) .... ISBN 0-8423-8268-2
The Scribe (Summer 2007) ....ISBN 0-8423-8269-0

Visit www.francinerivers.com